THE TROKEVILLE WAY

Also by Russell Hoban

THE MOUSE AND HIS CHILD

THE
TROKEVILLE WAY

Russell Hoban

Jonathan Cape
LONDON

For Tom

First published 1996

1 3 5 7 9 10 8 6 4 2

Copyright © 1996 Russell Hoban
Map © 1996 Patrick Benson

Russell Hoban has asserted his right
under the Copyright, Designs and Patents Act, 1988
to be identified as the author of this work

First published in Great Britain 1996
by Jonathan Cape
an imprint of Random House
20 Vauxhall Bridge Road, London SW1V 2SA

Random House Australia (Pty) Ltd
20 Alfred Street, Milsons Point, Sydney, NSW 2061, Australia

Random House New Zealand Ltd
18 Poland Road, Glenfield, Auckland, New Zealand

Random House South Africa (Pty) Ltd
PO Box 337, Bergvlei 2012, South Africa

Random House UK Limited Reg. No 954009

A CIP catalogue record for this book is
available from the British Library

ISBN 0224046314

Phototypeset by Intype, London
Printed and bound by
Mackays of Chatham PLC, Chatham, Kent

Contents

Acknowledgements

My youngest son, Wieland, was my consultant on school matters for this story, and both he and his brother, Ben, were kind enough to read and comment on various drafts.

R.H.

The author and publisher are indebted to Eaton Music Ltd for permission to quote from the song, *I've Seen That Face Before*. Copyright © 1981. Eaton Music Ltd.

But ere the circle homeward hies
Far, far must it remove . . .
                    A. E. Housman,
                    A Shropshire Lad

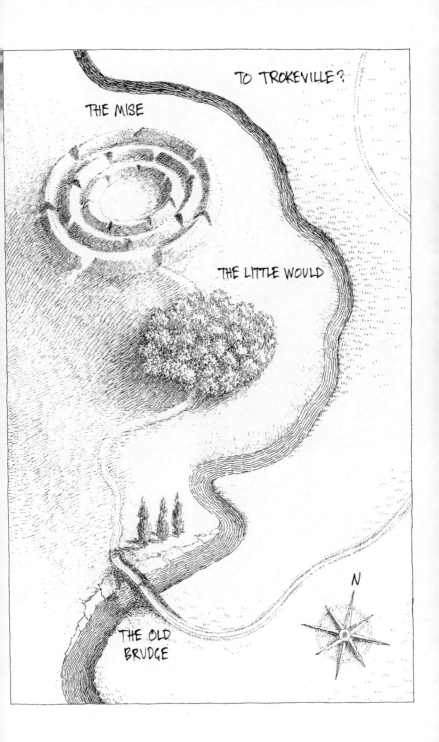

1

Moe Nagic

I met Moe Nagic four years ago when I was four months away from my thirteenth birthday. It was on a Monday in September in my last year at Castleford Court. In lunch break that day I had my third fight with Harry Buncher. I was leaning against the brick wall of the schoolyard, smelling the tomato sauce on my tie and thinking of all the school lunches still ahead of me when here came Buncher swinging his conker. With him were the boys who usually followed him around.

"Give you a game," he said, and winked at his hangers-on. With Buncher came his smell. I don't know whether it was that he didn't bath often enough or he sweated more than the rest of us or because his hormones were ahead of ours – whatever it was, he had a really depressing smell that took the heart out of you before anything even started.

My conker was a champion from the year before but I hadn't baked it or done anything else to it and I wasn't expecting it to last too much longer. Buncher's conker was glistening with varnish and it looked rock-hard. "I'll go first," he said. His conker smacked into mine and mine windmilled. "I get another go," he said. Another hard smack and both conkers bounced back with no windmilling.

"My go," I said. I could feel from my swing that it was going to be a winner and I smashed Buncher's conker to bits. A big quietness sprang up around us. Buncher was looking at me with his eyes all beady and his mouth shut tight and he was nodding his head as if he wouldn't have believed what treachery there was in the world but here was living proof of it.

"Let's have a look at that," he said. He grabbed my conker, swung it round his head, and smashed it against the wall. "Oh, dear," he said. "It wasn't all that hard, was it, Nicky boy." He laughed and looked around at his hangers-on who laughed obediently.

HERE WE GO AGAIN, said my mind. I heard a sigh coming out of me. "You bastard," I said to Buncher.

Buncher was pumping himself up now. He wasn't much in the classroom but he was great in the school-yard. "What did you call me?"

"What I said," I said, and got ready. I knew I was going to lose, the same as I'd lost the other two fights with him. Not because he was bigger, although he *was* bigger and a year older, but because I could never work up as much rage as he had in him all the time. He was like a boiling pot with its lid jumping up and down and he was pulling such horrible faces that I wondered how he could have stored up so much hate in the years of his life. He was so *serious* about the whole thing. Once he started pumping himself up for the fight he didn't care what happened – he didn't care if he got a month of detentions or if he got thrown out of school or if one or both of us ended up in hospital. He would win because all of him was out to win and all of me wasn't. Now here he was, looking horrendous and coming at me with that awful pong coming ahead of him. "You're asking for it," he said. He grabbed the front of my jumper and I hit him in the stomach with a good right.

"Oof!" he said, and doubled over. So far, so good, I thought, and I caught him on the side of the jaw with a left. Oh God, I thought, now he's really going to be mad. I backed away a little and when Buncher saw that he let out a roar and rushed me. I saw the top of his head as it smashed into my face and my head banged into the wall; there were fireworks and a sound like distant surf, then blackness and I disappeared for a while.

When I came to, there were Tom Jeffreys and Bill Wiggins, not part of Buncher's crowd, standing over me. Both of them were out of focus and at first I didn't hear what they were saying because of the roaring in my head but after a while that went away. "You're all bloody," said Tom. "Maybe we should get Matron." I shook my head, which didn't feel terribly good, and rubbed my eyes as Tom and Bill came into focus. I looked around at the schoolyard and everything seemed sharper and more detailed than usual; the red bricks, the grey slates on the roofs of the sheds, the trees beyond the wall – all of them had more colour in them than before. There was something like the memory of a smell in my mind, not the Buncher smell but something else. Then it was gone.

"I'm all right," I said. "I don't need Matron." Sometimes something happens and you know it's a special thing: whether it's bad or good doesn't matter – it's a thing that belongs to you in a special way.

3

"You were doing great until he headed you," said Bill.

"Ten seconds of greatness," I said. "Not quite enough." The back of my head was sticky with blood and there was a lump about the size of a cricket ball but I went to the lavatory and cleaned myself up and I was at my desk when the bell rang for the next class which was English. The lump on my head was throbbing like a disco, my head in general felt very strange, and my vision still had more colour and detail than I was used to but it was my thing and I was determined to stay with it. When Buncher came in with his crowd he said something to them and they all laughed and looked at me as they took their seats.

We didn't have a class reader then because we were spending most of our time swotting for Common Entrance. Our teacher, Mr Klein, however, used to read to us sometimes from works that he thought might put some heart into us. He was a small puny man with spectacles and he was bald on top. He loved to read us stories and poems about heroic deeds: we'd had Housman's poem about the Spartans who sat on the sea-wet rocks and combed their hair while waiting to be wiped out by the Persians at Thermopylae; and of course Macaulay's *Lays of Ancient Rome*. On this day he read us *Horatius*. You could see that it was a big emotional thing for him but we boys were realistic about fighting and we had a lot of trouble believing that three Romans could have held that bridge against the whole Tuscan army. Surely they could have been brought down by javelins? Still, it had a rousing sound to it:

4

"Hew down the bridge, Sir Consul,
  With all the speed ye may;
I, with two more to help me,
  Will hold the foe in play."

While Mr Klein's voice faded into the background of my consciousness my mind was saying, YOU COULD HAVE DONE BETTER AGAINST BUNCHER; HE'S EASY TO HIT.

I know.

THEN WHY DIDN'T YOU?

I was afraid of making him mad, that's why I backed away.

THAT WAS PRETTY STUPID, WASN'T IT? HE WAS ABOUT AS MAD AS HE COULD BE FROM THE VERY BEGINNING. AND HE CERTAINLY DIDN'T CARE ABOUT MAKING *YOU* MAD.

I know.

THEN WHY SHOULD YOU CARE ABOUT HIM?

I don't.

SO WHEN ARE YOU GOING TO STOP BACKING AWAY FROM BUNCHER? THIS YEAR, NEXT YEAR, SOMETIME, NEVER?

Sometime, I said. All right?

NO, IT'S NOT ALL RIGHT. TELL ME THIS: WHAT WOULD IT TAKE TO MAKE YOU WIN A FIGHT WITH BUNCHER?

I'd have to get mad enough not to care about making him mad.

IT'S THAT SIMPLE, IS IT? NO MAGIC REQUIRED – JUST GET MAD ENOUGH NOT TO CARE?

Yes, it's that simple.

REMEMBER THAT.

I'll remember, I said. My head still felt really weird but apparently I'd got through the rest of the school day because when I next looked down at my feet they were in the Castleford Road kicking a piece of broken glass along as I walked home. Again I noticed how sharp the picture in my eyes was and how intense the colours were. Whatever I looked at seemed more so than usual. The road was baking in the afternoon sun, the air was full of exhaust fumes. The estate agents' windows were full of overpriced houses and the adjective 'superb'; the antique-shop windows were full of things that nobody but another dealer would buy; the pavement was full of feet, elbows, and loud voices from The Green Man. Vaporised grease from McDonald's was inviting lovers of dead meat; hardfaced dog-owners stared into the distance while their pets fouled the footpath; and sweaty boys and girls bulging with satchels, sports bags, and hormones went slouching towards home trailing cigarette smoke and swear words.

I was passing a hoarding where there used to be a parade of shops and now there were only graffiti and posters for rock groups. There was a man sitting on the pavement with his back against the hoarding and he was playing a concertina. What stopped me was the music he was playing: it was a spooky, shadowy-sounding thing I'd heard years ago at the circus during a trapeze act. A kind of darkness came into the light and I could see the bright spangled figures high up in the rigging of the tent, I could feel in my stomach the rush of danger when they let go and flew through the air to the hands that caught them. They had a net below them but the net made me think: what if there were no net? And the sinister music reinforced that thought. Dad had that music on a CD with a vocal by Grace Jones, *'I've Seen That Face Before'*:

Strange – I've seen that face before,
seen him hanging round my door,
like a hawk feeling for the prey,
like a night waiting for the day.

There was an upturned baseball cap on the pavement beside the man with some coins in it so I dropped in 10p and he nodded to me and went on playing. There were things next to him that he was evidently selling but it was the music that kept me there; it seemed somehow to be beckoning. As I stood listening his elbows stopped going in and out and the music died. The darkness went away and it was like coming out of a Saturday-afternoon cinema and blinking in the sunlight.

"What?" he said.

"Sorry?"

"What's on your mind?" His voice was low and gravelly, almost a whisper. His eyes were fixed on me in a way that made me wonder if he was a hypnotist. They were grey eyes, large and luminous, sad and mysterious. Strange – it seemed to me I'd seen those eyes before.

"The music," I said.

" '*Libertango*' by Astor Piazzola. What about it?"

"Reminded me of the circus."

"Something dangerous?"

"Trapeze artists."

"Ah!" He was wearing faded denim trousers with holes in the knees, worn-out trainers, and a dirty white T-shirt. I guessed he was sixty or so: medium height, grey hair, bald on top, a face that might have been handsome once. Looked as if he'd been sleeping rough or possibly not sleeping at all.

7

He had a small flat bottle of whisky in a paper bag beside him with his little huddle of merchandise. There were a few books, some of them, by the style of their covers, quite old but all of them looking mostly unread: *Self-Defence for Everybody*; *Do It to Them Before They Do It to You*; *Ten Steps to a More Powerful Body*; *Fifty Classic Card Tricks*; *Zen in the Art of Archery*; *The Myth of Sisyphus*; *The Primal Scream*; and *Teach Yourself Concertina*. There was a Bullworker with its exercise manual; there was a stringless gyroscope. Leant against the hoarding was a fully-assembled jigsaw puzzle, about twenty by thirty centimetres. It was in a shallow wooden box that seemed specially made for it. Looking closer I saw that it was a watercolour that had been glued to a backing and jig-sawed into a puzzle. Odd sort of thing to do to a water-colour, I thought. On the edge of the box was a gummed label, hand-lettered: THE TROKEVILLE WAY. Just above it was a poster for a group called Revelation.

THE TROKEVILLE WAY, said my mind.

What?

NOTHING, I JUST SAID, 'THE TROKEVILLE WAY.'

What about it?

WELL, LET'S SEE, SHALL WE? NO HARM IN LOOKING, IS THERE?

That's right, all I'm doing is looking.

RIGHT, I'LL LEAVE YOU TO IT.

There was no name or date on the picture but it didn't look very old and I guessed it had been done in the last twenty years. The main thing in it was an old stone bridge over a little river; the shadow of the bridge was on the water under the arch and there was ivy growing up the sides of the stonework; various rocks and bushes and a tree in the foreground; three trees on the left bank could be seen through the arch – they looked like three girls going down to the river for a swim. In the distance beyond them, rather dim, was a hill with a little wood on top of it. There were two figures on the bridge, just their heads and shoulders showing above the parapet, very vague and shadowy: they might have been any two people of either sex. It was summer in the picture, the trees in full leaf. The whole scene was full of that light you get before a thunderstorm. One of the figures on the bridge seemed to be looking towards me and I felt that he or she was waiting for me to make a move. The bridge, the trees, the sky, the river – everything seemed to be waiting. "Where's Trokeville?" I said to the man.

"You know," he said, "since I got here at half-past two there've been twenty-seven people past here and you're the only one who's asked me that."

"So where is it?"

"You can't see it from here, you have to get into the picture."

"I mean, is it in England or Scotland or what?"

"Nothing like that, I told you – you have to get into the picture."

"Is *The Trokeville Way* a method or a road?"

"It's a road."

"Does it go across the bridge?"

"Brudge. Yes, it goes across the brudge."

"Did you say 'brudge'?"

"That's what I said."

"That's a funny way of saying bridge."

"I'm a funny sort of guy."

"You still haven't said where Trokeville is."

"Why are you so keen to know? Have you got business there?"

"If you call this picture *The Trokeville Way* then surely you must expect someone to ask you where Trokeville is."

"That's hard to say. You can see it when you're in the picture."

"You keep saying that. What would I have to do to get into this picture?"

STEADY ON, said my mind.

"Why would you want to?" said the man.

"I'm not saying I want to, I'm just asking how I'd do it if I *did* want to."

"Slow down, you've got your whole life ahead of you."

"Good job I have because it's taking quite a long time to get a couple of simple answers out of you."

"Simple answers are very rare. Bet you can't guess my name."

"Rumpelstiltskin?"

"Moe Nagic. There's no magic but there's Moe Nagic. How about that?"

"I guess that's how it is."

"What's your name?"

"Nick Hartley."

"You know something, Nick –"

"Not yet."

"How old are you?"

"Almost thirteen."

"I'm forty-seven. Whatever you're doing, when you're

my age you'll think of how you could have done it better."

"Right this minute I'm thinking of how I could have done it better."

"Are you! You're a deep one, I can see that. Have a look at this." He took a folded-up piece of paper out of his pocket and unfolded it and gave it to me. It was a very old handbill coming apart at the creases and on it was a photograph of a much younger man in white tie and tails with a beautiful young woman wearing not much except sequins and fishnet tights and a brilliant smile. Under the photo it said:

*************** BRIGHTON PIER ***************
THE AMAZING MORRIS NAGIC AND ZELDA
Appearing nightly 14 July – 1 August

"You?" I said.

He nodded.

"What did you do?"

"Illusions. Made people think they were seeing what they weren't – sawed Zelda in half, made her disappear, made myself disappear and reappear in odd places, that sort of thing. The most magical part of it was the atmosphere, everything all sparkly and special and us in the spotlight and the band playing that tango I was doing when you came along. It's got mystery, that music, it's got magic – it takes you out of the everyday sameness into a place where anything can happen. People crave that, you know: they want to believe in the extra-real and I used to give them the illusion of it. How do you feel about reality?"

"Well, what else is there?"

"I'll be more specific. This reality that we're in – do you think it's the only one?"

"It's the only one I know of."

"Lucky you. But we were talking about me and Zelda. One evening right after the show she said to me – and she was still in costume, looking absolutely ravishing when she said it – 'Moe, the Nagic has gone out of it for me.' She always had a sense of humour. 'I'm leaving you for Charles,' she said. Just like that. I felt as if she'd sawed me in half. Charles was the opposite of a disappearing act: all of a sudden, out of nowhere, he appeared. Charles was a reality man, no illusions, hard facts, a chartered accountant. Never put your trust in a woman named Zelda."

"I'll remember that."

"Remember this too: winners get what they want and losers get what they deserve. 'You won't be happy with Charles,' I told her. By then we were outside, in front of Mrs Whitby's Seaview Hotel; Zelda was all packed and ready to go and Charles pulled up in his Jaguar. 'There won't be any magic with him,' I said. 'Magic!' he said. 'Look at you, with your pathetic little tricks and your bed-and-breakfasts! You call that magic?' As well as the Jaguar he had a house in Welwyn Garden City.

" 'You've got no soul,' I said to him. Because he didn't and she knew it. He wasn't the sort of man who would ever wake her up to watch the sun rise over the sea. She was looking from him to me and maybe wavering a little as she saw him through the eyes of how she used to be.

" 'Don't leave me, Zelda,' I said. I grabbed her and

12

Charles knocked me down. I got up and went for him and he knocked me down again. He wasn't any bigger than I was and I doubt that he was any fitter – he just seemed to be madder than I was. We went at it until he knocked me down again, my head hit the kerb, and I was out like a light. When I opened my eyes the smell of Charles's exhaust was still hanging in the air but he and Zelda were gone.

"The lump on my head was throbbing, I felt very strange, and there was too much colour, too much detail in whatever I looked at. And smells – I still remember the smell of that Jaguar's exhaust. Since then I've been a failure. I taught myself to play the concertina and I play music that's full of darkness. This one's called '*Fear*'." His hand on the concertina seemed very thin and I noticed nicotine stains on his fingers. He played something that made me see the shine of street lamps on wet cobblestones and a figure hurrying down a dark alley and looking back over his shoulder. "Can't get away from it," he said. "I wake up in the morning and I say to myself, 'Here comes another day of being a failure.'" He put down the concertina in a very sad and careful way, like a man taking off his spectacles before jumping off a tall building. "Do you understand what I'm saying?"

"Yes."

IT'S NOT TOO LATE TO WALK AWAY FROM THIS, said my mind.

"Know what it is to be a failure, do you?" said Moe Nagic. He pulled a crushed and mostly used-up ounce of Golden Virginia and a packet of papers out of his pocket, rolled a cigarette, lit it, took a deep drag, and blew out a cloud of smoke that smelled like the music he'd just played.

"Yes," I said, "I know what it is to be a failure."

"What about winning? Done much winning?"

"Not a lot."

"Think you could?"

"I don't know."

"Think winning, it's better than losing."

"I'll try."

"Yes, try. Where was I?"

"Smelling the Jaguar's exhaust."

"Right. I went up to our room at the Seaview then, Zelda's and mine. I stood there in the dark smelling her perfume for a while; then I turned on the light and the empty room stared back at me. I don't know why but my eye fell on one particular empty space right over the bed. When we took the room there was a framed watercolour hanging there, *The Old Brudge* was the title written on the matt in pencil: not *Bridge* but *Brudge*. It was the first thing that caught Zelda's eye when we came into the room. She put down the bags she was carrying and just stood looking at it. I said to her, 'What's a brudge?' and she said. 'A bridge with a grudge, I suppose. That picture gives me the creeps.' 'Why?' I said. 'I don't know,' she said, 'it just does. Please take it down and put it where I don't have to see it.' I'd put it in the cupboard but now with Zelda gone something made me hang it up again for a closer look. We weren't married – we'd said we'd cross that bridge when we came to it, and I wondered if that had had anything to do with her dislike of the picture.

"I still wasn't feeling myself or maybe I was more

14

myself than I'd ever been, I'm not sure which. I took off my shoes and stood on the bed – it was an old-fashioned brass bed with railings and knobs at the head and foot. I held on to the headrail, not feeling too steady, and I stared at that picture, that bridge I hadn't crossed. I'd never really looked at it closely before but this time I felt that I needed to know more about it. Have I said it was unsigned? Well, it was, and I wondered about that. Maybe it was that knock on the head – I don't know – but my mind seemed to be in a whole new place and the picture was getting real for me: by moving my head I could see more of what was beyond the bridge or brudge and I was taking it in with all my senses. I was leaning closer to the picture, leaning into it, then all of a sudden I was *in* it, something like Alice going through the looking-glass – I was in that place with the brudge and the river but it wasn't the way it looked from the outside – that river was black and it stank. I heard the rush of it and the wind in the trees. It was twilight where I was, that eerie kind of twilight you get before a thunderstorm but darker than it'd looked in the picture, and the leaves were pattering and showing their under-sides the way they do before rain. You're looking at me with a question in your face: why am I telling you all this, right?"

"Right."

"Because you heard what was in the music and you asked me about *The Trokeville Way*, which must mean something. And because I need to. Have you got a prob-lem with that?"

"No, please go on."

"The rocks in the foreground – I touched them, I mean

15

I could actually feel them with my fingers, the rocks and the moss on them. On the left bank of the river, past those three trees, there was a hill with a little wood on the top of it – you can see that in the put-together puzzle but you can't see the lights of a town that I saw in the distance on the right bank when I moved my head to the left."

"Trokeville?"

He nodded. "All the while this was happening I knew that I was standing on a bed in our room in Mrs Whitby's Seaview Hotel. I wasn't out of touch with reality – I was in touch with *two* realities."

"Two realities!"

"Is that so hard to take in? You look like a clever boy; think about it – maybe there's more than one level, more than one layer of reality. Maybe if you peel the top layer off you'll find another layer underneath. And maybe that's where the real action is. You understand what I'm saying? Being almost thirteen doesn't come into it – either you've got the feeling for it or you haven't."

"I've got it." When I said that I wasn't dead sure about it but I knew that I *wanted* to have it.

He held out his hand. I shook it, and I knew then that we were in it together, whatever it was. "Why did you cut up that picture and make a puzzle out of it?" I said.

"Because it only does what it does when it's all together and I needed to be able to stop it sometimes."

"Stop what?"

He looked at me for a while without saying anything, as if he was deciding whether or not I was up to whatever he was thinking of. "Do you want to try it? Do you want to get into that picture just for a moment or two?

16

I promise you'll get back safely in less than a couple of minutes."

STILL NOT TOO LATE TO WALK AWAY, said my mind.

"OK," I said to Moe Nagic, "I'll try it. What do I have to do?"

"Have you got a piece of string?"

"Yes."

"Destiny. This was meant to happen. You believe that?"

"I don't know."

"Yes, you do." He picked up the gyroscope and handed it to me. "This is just something to get you focused on what you're doing. Give it a spin and when you see the words WAY IN on the flywheel you just sort of lean into the picture."

"How do I get out again?"

"When the gyroscope stops you're out. One thing to remember: this is your first time and you're only doing a quick recce. The puzzle is what I call a juzzle . . ."

"Why?"

"I don't know. Maybe when I first started with it I didn't want to call things by their right names. If you were to get into this seriously there might come later what I call a troke or maybe not . . ."

"What's a troke?"

"I think of it as partly a trick and partly a stroke. But for now you're just thinking juzzle and putting yourself in the picture but you're not to get into any kind of action this trip, OK?"

"OK." I didn't ask what kind of action he meant. I knelt on the pavement about two feet from the juzzle. My head was still feeling strange and my vision was definitely not the usual thing; when I looked at the gyroscope I seemed to be seeing it through a magnifying glass and separate from the world around it. The two intersecting outer rings and the spindle were shiny; the flywheel was a dull grey with blue and red markings on it; I noticed that the metal was pitted here and there.

NOW IT'S TOO LATE, said my mind.

I wound the string round the spindle, held the north and south poles of it between the thumb and index finger of my right hand, and pulled with my left. As the flywheel spun I saw shimmering purple letters that said WAY IN.

I set the spinning gyroscope down on my Geometry book as the sounds of the Castleford Road faded out and a silence flowed in all around me. I leant into the picture and then I was standing in it, standing on the old brudge. Moe Nagic was there as well; we were the two figures in the picture. The gyroscope was spinning on the stone parapet. I smelled the river before I saw it, heard it too – it made a hissing sound. I looked down at it, black and moving fast and not like water at all. The air was heavy and full of dread – that's the only word I can think of for it. When I spoke my voice seemed to be sounding only in my head. "This isn't real, is it?" I said to Moe Nagic.

"Not in the usual way." His voice sounded the same. He slapped the parapet. "First-class stonework. They don't build them like this any more."

"But it's all in my head, wouldn't you say?"

"So is everything else. I mean, if you turn off your head the whole world goes away, doesn't it?"

"Yes." The gyroscope stopped spinning; for a moment

it lay still on the parapet, then the old stone brudge was gone. I was kneeling in front of the juzzle and Moe Nagic was sitting on the pavement with his back against the hoarding, drinking from his bagged bottle. The gyroscope had fallen off the Geometry book on to the pavement.

I've said before that my head felt strange but that word doesn't describe exactly how it was – turbocharged would be closer to it.

"What do you think?" said Moe Nagic.

"I don't know what to think."

"Go on, be straight with me – I've been straight with you."

"Have you?"

"More or less."

"Maybe less?"

"What're you talking about?"

"You seem to want me to get involved with this juzzle and you said there wasn't to be any action just now when we did the recce. What kind of action might there be another time?"

"That depends on you – if you decide to try it another time, that is."

"With you, you mean?"

"Oh no, it's a thing you'll have to do alone."

"But there are two figures on the bridge."

"Probably somebody will turn up once you're there."

"Who?"

"As I said, it depends on you."

"How would it depend on me?"

"There's no magic, remember? The whole thing is a mind trip. It's a level of reality that you get to with your mind and it's your mind that determines whom and what you encounter. I feel morally obliged to tell you one thing, though – you get into that picture and you'll wish you were out of it."

"Why?"

"Life is like that, isn't it. You get into something and you wish you were out of it."

"Could I get stuck in there and never get out again?"

"If you've got a dangerous mind there could be danger. If you're afraid maybe you'd better forget it."

"I'm not afraid."

"Then stop asking afraid questions or I'll begin to think you're a loser."

I'd noticed that my mind hadn't been saying anything for a while. What about it? I said. Are you dangerous?

WHAT DO *YOU* THINK?

I'm afraid to say.

THERE'S YOUR ANSWER.

O God, I thought. How did I get into this? Just a few minutes ago it wasn't happening and now there seems to be no way back.

THERE NEVER IS, said my mind.

"What about the troke?" I said to Moe Nagic. "Where does that come into it?"

"I can't say for sure – I never managed it."

"Great. That's really terrific. What kind of trick or stroke *is* the troke anyhow?"

"I believe it's the trick or stroke that gets you to Trokeville."

"And you never managed it."

"I told you – I'm a failure." He paused for a quick

20

drink, rolled another cigarette, lit it, inhaled, blew out smoke, and looked into the distance.

"So you never got to Trokeville," I said.

"That's right. I've seen it from a distance like Moses looking at the land of Canaan but I never got there."

"How much do you want for the juzzle and the gyroscope?"

"How much have you got?"

"Two pounds forty-two p."

"Done." He took the juzzle apart, put the pieces in the box, closed the box, shook it three times, then gave it to me with the gyroscope. He said, "You might find it helpful to think of the things in that place by the names I use. The things are off straight so I gave them off-straight names and you should think of them off straight. There's the old brudge of course, and if you cross that in the direction I think you'll take you'll come to the little wood which is the little *would*, spelled W-O-U-L-D; beyond the little would, not visible from the brudge, there's a maze which I call a *mise*, M-I-S-E."

"Why do you call it a mise?"

"Just my fancy, that's all. I call the town *Trokeville* because I'm pretty sure you can only get to it if you've done the troke. I don't want to tell you any more because I'd rather not clutter your mind with my experience – in any case it'll all be different for you. It was easy for you to get into the picture today because you were with me. When you do it alone you might find it more diffi-cult. Another thing – be careful with the gyroscope when you're in the juzzle. I haven't used it for years because after a while I could just slip in and out without any gimmicks but while you're learning it's best if the gyro spins until it stops by itself; it shouldn't be interfered with."

"What could happen?"

"I don't know. This is not a no-risk kind of thing."

"One more thing: why are you selling the juzzle and the gyro?"

"Because enough's enough, OK? Are you buying or not?"

"I'm buying." I gave him all the money I had in my pocket and we shook hands again. "Think winning," he said. He waved goodbye, picked up the concertina, and began playing '*Libertango*' again.

2

The Old Brudge

The next time I looked down at my feet I was standing in our kitchen with the juzzle box under my arm. It was like a film where they cut from one scene to the next with nothing in between. My head still felt turbocharged and I didn't know if that was because of Moe Nagic or Harry Buncher. Mum was standing in front of me with her mouth moving and after a while the sound came on. ". . . Your head?" she said.

"Ran wackwards into a ball, backwards into a wall frying to catch a trisbee, frisbee in the schoolyard."

"Did you knock yourself out? Were you unconscious at all?"

"No." I didn't want to be examined by a doctor, didn't want the turbocharged feeling to be taken away from me. She dragged me off to the bathroom, cleaned the wound, ascertained that it was a bad scrape but nothing requiring stitches, swabbed it with TCP, rummaged in a drawer till she found her list that showed when I'd had my last tetanus shot, then turned me loose.

When I got to my room I closed the door and put the juzzle box on my desk. I took the gyroscope out of my satchel and put that on the desk as well. It just looked like any old banged-up gyroscope. I opened the juzzle box and looked at the pieces and this time it struck me that all the other jigsaw puzzles I'd ever seen looked harmless and this one didn't.

My mind said to me, WELL, WHAT DO YOU THINK? ARE YOU READY FOR THE OLD BRUDGE, THE LITTLE WOULD, AND THE MISE? WILL YOU BE UP TO DOING THE TROKE?

I don't know, I said. I looked around my room as if I were saying goodbye to it. From my brother David's room I could hear the sound of Gaye Bikers on Acid and from downstairs 'Claire de Lune' drifting up from Mum's piano. She'd only recently got the piece and she played it hesitantly. Leaning against my pillow on the patchwork bedspread she'd crocheted were my worn-out teddy bear and frazzled crocodile and four or five other old friends, all looking at me as if from long ago. The guitar I'd got for my birthday was leaning against the wall in a corner; my flute was on top of the chest of drawers and my flute certificates were on the wall along with Iron Maiden, Morgoth, and Sepultura posters. I'm listening to a Bartok quartet as I write this and the time when I had ears for that other music seems a long way back.

The juzzle and the gyroscope were waiting on my desk but I wasn't ready yet. "Later," I said. I didn't feel like hearing any music then so I just sat there and listened to the humming in my head until dinner time.

At the table I found myself sitting with people who suddenly looked as if I'd never seen them before. The one called Mum said, "How's your head?"

"Fine."

24

"Any reason why it shouldn't be?" said the one called Dad.

"Ran backwards into a wall trying to catch a frisbee in the schoolyard," I said.

"Did you!" said Dad, in a way that invited me to pull the other one. Then he and Mum got talking about what kind of a day each of them had had. I found myself thinking of Moe Nagic and Zelda, how he'd become a failure after losing her to Charles the chartered accountant. He shouldn't have given up so easily, I said to myself.

LOOK WHO'S TALKING, said my mind.

"Why? Did you have an especially bad one?" said Dad to me.

"What?" I said.

"Day," said Dad. "I said I'd had a really rotten day and you said, 'Look who's talking'."

"Sorry, I didn't realise I was speaking out loud. I was just replaying a conversation in my head – nothing to do with what you were saying."

"*Did* you have a bad day, though?" said Mum. "Apart from the lump on your head you don't quite look yourself."

"It was just a normal day except that I ran into a wall."

"Could happen to anyone," said Dad. "Sometimes walls turn up where you least expect them." Then he went into tremendous detail about his bad day which included a row with his boss and a rise in interest rates at the building society where he works.

"Raising the interest rates is like putting an elastoplast on a corpse," said David. He was doing A Levels and being a Marxist and wearing a Dead Kennedys T-shirt with a rude slogan.

Dad of course rose to the bait immediately. "It's easy to sneer," he said.

"Must everything be difficult?" said David. He made one or two other remarks that made the vein in Dad's forehead begin to throb and a brisk exchange of views developed between the two of them.

By the time we'd got through the Dad-and-David debate and pudding and cleared the table and loaded the dishwasher it was quarter past eight. Dad disappeared into his PC, David rang up a few fellow-Marxists to organise some fly-posting, and I practised my Bach flute sonata while Mum listened. Then finally I was alone with the juzzle and the gyroscope in my room.

So there we were. The lump on my head was throbbing as if it were broadcasting my thoughts to the world. I seemed to have stopped breathing out but even so I let out a big breath, rubbed my hands together and said, "Well, here we are." After that there was nothing left but to get started.

I had a four-foot by four-foot piece of hardboard that I used when I had big drawings or maps to do so I laid it on the floor and spilled the pieces of the juzzle on to it and started turning them all right-side up. By the time I'd done that it was quarter-past nine and I had to get started on my Geometry prep. When Mum and Dad came in to kiss me goodnight at half-past nine I hadn't finished the Geometry and there were the juzzle pieces all spread out on the floor. "Have you got time for that?" said Mum.

"Just a little relaxation between preps," I said. "Only a few minutes now and then."

"That puzzle doesn't seem quite the usual thing," said Dad. He knelt for a closer look. "It's an original watercolour someone's cut up! What an act of vandalism! Who'd do a thing like that?"

"I bought it from a man in the Castleford Road," I said.

"I'd like to see it when you get it put together," said Dad.

"Right," I said. I didn't really want him to get too interested. I was feeling quite uneasy and I needed something pleasant to send me off to sleep so I thought about Tom Jeffreys' fourteen-year-old sister, Cynthia. She looked like the girl in a painting I'd seen at the Tate, *King Cophetua and the Beggar Maid* by Burne-Jones. The beggar maid is wearing what looks like a clinging black nightie that leaves a lot of her bare. The King is sitting at her feet, entranced. Beautiful feet of course, with the second toe longer than the big toe. Her great luminous eyes are open wide and she's looking not at him but straight ahead. She too seems entranced, perhaps by her own beauty. To me her face always seemed full of terror and mystery and sadness. Being a king, Cophetua could pick her out of a crowd of beggars and do what he liked with her but I wondered if he was equal to what I saw in her face.

Sometimes when I was at the Jeffreys' house visiting Tom I'd hear Cynthia talking on the telephone in the hall or she'd come and look over my shoulder when Tom and I were playing chess and I'd smell her hair. I hadn't ever talked to her really and I sometimes used to try to think of what I might say if we ever did talk but the words always sounded stupid. Lying in bed that night I tried to make up a little poem about her. The furthest I got was:

> Upon this old brudge under thundery skies,
> alone I stand, and little would surmise . . .

Surmise! I thought. When had I ever used *that* word? And yet it had a familiar ring: would surmise, would surmise . . . *Wild* surmise. I'd heard that somewhere: *'Speechless in wild surmise upon a peak in Darien'*. Not quite. Ah! Mr Klein had read it to us: it was Keats, *On First Looking into Chapman's Homer*. I switched on the lamp, got *The Dragon Book of Verse* off my bedside shelf and found the poem. The lines I wanted were:

> Or like stout Cortez when with eagle eyes
> He star'd at the Pacific – and all his men
> Looked at each other with a wild surmise –
> Silent, upon a peak in Darien.

I put the book back on the shelf, switched off the lamp, closed my eyes, and from my high peak saw the blue Pacific sparkling in the sun. So wide and far and blue, so deep and unknown! Full of wild surmise about many, many things I drifted off to sleep.

I dreamt that I was putting the juzzle together and I was amazed at how quickly it went; sometimes it seemed that the right pieces were jumping into my hand when I wasn't even looking at them. The shapes, I noticed, weren't quite like those of ordinary jigsaws,

28

there was something sly and knowing about them. My head still felt turbocharged but I couldn't be certain because sometimes I thought it must always have been like that: I saw things in a special way and I understood them in a special way. It began to seem to me that the juzzle had a life of its own – it wanted to come together, whether for itself or me I didn't know. As the old brudge took shape the whole thing started to get heavy for me; I resented being hurried along by that dreary picture but I couldn't stop putting it together.

Suddenly the picture was complete and the scene with the old brudge was waiting for me to move into it. Right, I said to myself. Here we go. I felt full of breath so I let it out, picked up the gyroscope, set the bottom of the spindle on the hardboard, and gave the string a strong pull.

WAY IN, said the shimmering purple letters. I leant towards the old brudge and it seemed to be leaning towards me; then suddenly I couldn't see, couldn't hear, couldn't breathe. I was drowning as if waters had closed over my head but it wasn't water, it was . . . what? The past? The present? O God! I thought, maybe this is the end of me. There was nothing like this when I got into the picture with Moe Nagic – that's what I get for trying it alone. Why had I wanted . . .? What had I wanted? I couldn't remember; everything was nothing.

Then I was on the brudge, alone. The spinning gyroscope was on the parapet. It didn't look safe there so I carefully moved it, still spinning, down to the stone roadway of the brudge. Where was the other figure? I couldn't see very well – it was as if I was looking at everything through a lens smeared with Vaseline. And yet there were details that were very clear: lichens on the stones of the brudge and leaves on distant trees seemed to be inches from my face. Everything had a loneliness about it, the way the world must have looked at the beginning, when there were no people and the first rains filled up the oceans. The sky was rumbling with thunder and flickering with lightning. The air was greenish, the stench from the black river almost took my breath away. My veins and arteries seemed to be filled with lead.

That thundery twilight seemed to be holding its breath and everything I looked at was quivering a little as if it might suddenly let go and disappear. Although the spinning of the gyroscope had put me into this picture I could feel that what I saw was only there because my mind wanted it to be there; I was afraid to hold on to it and I was afraid to let go. What would there be if I let go? The drowning again? The fact that my own mind was doing this was the scariest thing about it.

What is this? I said to it. Whose side are you on?

I'M WHAT THERE IS, I'M THE WORLD THAT LIVES IN YOUR HEAD.

Is that all you can say?

THAT'S ALL THERE IS TO SAY. HOW ABOUT LESS TALK AND MORE ACTION?

My mind and I had been talking to each other for as long as I could remember and I was used to its manner but I could have done with a little more support just then. As it was, all I could do was try to be strong until the gyroscope stopped spinning and I was home again.

I was exactly in the middle of the brudge, directly over the middle of the river. On the left bank were the three trees that had looked like girls going down to the river for a swim, but now they were more like three tall blind things stretching out their arms towards me. Beyond them I saw the hill with the little would; the trees were huddled together in a way that made an emptiness all around them and they looked as if they mightn't be trees the next time I looked – they were misshapen and the spaces between them seemed to twist and move. There was an uphill slant to the brudge on that side.

On the right bank the roadway led on to a track across a plain. There were the lights of a town far away: Trokeville. Had anyone ever reached it or was it just a mind-mirage that was part of this picture-world? Given the choice in situations where it makes no difference I tend to go left; here it very likely would make a big difference. In any case left felt like the way to go – it was the way Moe Nagic had expected me to go and uphill seemed more likely to earn a result than downhill so I faced left. Maybe later there'd be another crossing to Trokeville. Maybe the distant lights were actually on the left bank of the river; it was hard to be certain but left felt right.

ALL RIGHT? said my mind. LET'S GO.

Still standing in the middle of the brudge I became aware of the rushing of the river. Being very careful not to kick the gyroscope I went to the parapet and looked down. What flowed under the brudge was black and smooth and shining and moving very fast. It didn't look like water and it smelled like a blocked drain. I felt the dread and the deep fear in my guts. What was there to be afraid of? I didn't know, so being afraid of everything seemed to make sense. From the little would I heard the hooting of an owl and the answering kee-wick. Two owls hunting. I tried to make myself very small and still, I didn't want to think of moving from where I was.

COME ON, said my mind, PULL YOURSELF TOGETHER.

I don't like it here. Why did I come here? I want to go back.

DON'T BE SUCH A BABY. YOU'RE THE ONE WHO WANTED TO DO THIS, SO DO IT.

Very faintly I could hear the music of 'Libertango' and Grace Jones singing:

> "Strange – I've seen that face before
> seen him hanging round my door . . ."

I felt myself letting go and the scene in front of me began to fade into a grey nothingness from the edges inward; soon there was nothing left but the part of the brudge I was standing on; then that was gone as well and I was drowning in the stinking blackness under the brudge. Then I woke up.

From the room Dad called his office I could hear, very faintly, Grace Jones singing, ". . . I've seen that face before." He hadn't listened to that for a long time; why was he playing it now? I looked at my clock and it was only a little after eleven. I tried to go back to sleep but I couldn't so I thought I might as well start on the juzzle. I switched on my bedside lamp and got out of bed. The juzzle was where I'd left it when I finished turning the pieces right-side up but it was completely assembled. The motionless gyroscope lay on it.

What is this? I said to my mind. Did I do it in my sleep or what?

WHAT'S THE DIFFERENCE? THE OLD BRUDGE IS READY WHEN YOU ARE.

What are you talking about? I've just been there!

FOR HOW LONG – TEN SECONDS?

It seemed longer.

NOT GOOD ENOUGH.

I did the best I could.

NO, YOU DIDN'T.

You were there, you must have felt how bad it was.

YOU'RE THE ONE WHO WANTED TO DO IT.

Did I ever say that in so many words? Did I ever actually say, "I want to do it"? I don't remember saying those words.

PLEASE, I'M EMBARRASSED FOR YOU AND I'D RATHER NOT HAVE THIS CONVERSATION. IF YOU DON'T LIKE WHERE THIS TRAIN IS GOING MAYBE YOU SHOULD GET OFF, OK?

All right, I'll go to the old brudge. Just tell me, though – *was* it a dream the last time?

DOESN'T MATTER – YOU'VE GOT TO DO BETTER.

So either for the first or second time that night I spun the gyroscope, drowned in blackness for a while, and got on to the brudge. Same feeling of dread, same thundery-looking sky, same stench from the river, same owls, same stillness and quivering in everything. My vision too was the same – like looking through a smeared lens but with odd patches of telescopic clarity. Again I was the only one on the brudge. I put the gyroscope on the roadway by the base of the parapet, then with my eyes on the little would I moved forward.

A silence sprang up around me; I could feel it pressing on my face in the twilight. In that little clump of trees on the hill I saw a glimmer of something, a white dress moving through the dimness. It was Cynthia Jeffreys, even at that distance I recognised her. Was she in danger? What was she doing in this place? In wild surmise I saw the blue Pacific sparkling in the sun. What? I said to my mind.

NOTHING.

I began to run but Harry Buncher loomed up in front of me.

"You!" I said. I was hearing my voice inside my head but I didn't know if it was making a sound anywhere else.

Buncher looked strange and pale and his lips were moving but no sound was coming out. "You!" he was saying. He was passing his hand back and forth in front of his face the way you do when you want something to go away and I was doing the same.

Shit! I said to my mind. Give a break, for God's sake!

DON'T BLAME ME, it said. THIS IS YOUR LIFE.

I tried to see past Buncher, tried to see the glimmer of white in the little would but I could feel myself letting go the same as the last time. Everything faded into grey from the edges inward until Buncher and the brudge were gone. I did the drowning in the blackness and then I was back in my room. The gyroscope was lying on the juzzle and the old brudge stared out of the picture at me. It was a little after eleven and Grace Jones was singing, "Strange – I've seen that face before." Am I awake now or asleep or what? I said to my mind.

WHAT'S THE DIFFERENCE?

I *knew* it was going to say that. I began to think about the gyroscope. Moe Nagic had explained that it was only something to get me focused on what I was doing, and when it stopped spinning I'd be out of the juzzle world. When I had the letting-go feeling, was that because the gyroscope was losing its spin? Or did the gyroscope lose its spin when I couldn't endure the juzzle world any longer? I said to my mind, Which is it?

I'M NOT SURE. WE HAVEN'T DONE IT ENOUGH TIMES FOR ME TO KNOW.

Then I tried to remember the sequence of events that had brought me to wherever I was now but I fell asleep while doing it.

Faint Music

When I woke up next morning I did a mental replay of the scene with Buncher on the brudge: he'd looked so pale, so *scared*. The mighty Buncher! He'd been just as scared as I was. At school I saw him in the hall on the way to class; he was alone and seemed thoughtful. When he saw me he said, "What are you looking at?"

NOTHING VERY MUCH, said my mind.

"Say that again?" said Buncher, pumping himself up.

"I never said anything the first time."

He shook his head as if to clear it. "Don't you come it with me," he said, and turned away and moved on, looking not quite as sure of himself as usual. In the schoolyard during lunch break he had his regular followers with him but he never looked in my direction and he wasn't bullying anyone else.

After school I was hoping to see Moe Nagic; he must have gone into the world of the old brudge many times and I wanted to hear how many tries it had taken for him to get across it and what had happened in the little would and the mise and the rest of it. He'd said that he'd never managed to do the troke himself but I wanted to know how close he'd come to it, how far he'd got on the road to Trokeville. Other things I wanted to know as well: he'd said that he'd been a failure from the time Zelda left him but I couldn't believe he'd simply got up the next morning and gone to fail the same as you'd go to work. Probably there'd been several stages from partial failure to total failure and I wanted to hear about them.

When I reached the spot that I now thought of as Moe Nagic's pitch everything was as it usually was: the drinkers were doing their thing outside The Green Man and the dog-owners and their pets were doing their thing on the footpath; McDonald's was putting out its usual scent signals; the estate agents were offering their many superbnesses; the antique-shop windows were talking to one another; the boys and girls were hormonising and smoking their way home – the scene was complete except for a big emptiness where Moe Nagic had been the day before. I felt that emptiness like a kick in the stomach. About this time yesterday he'd been nothing at all to me but now his absence made me feel as if I'd been deserted. There were so many things I wanted to ask him and here he was – gone! O God! I said to myself, I'm all alone with it.

THAT'S WHAT LIFE IS, said my mind. GET USED TO IT.

Thanks a lot, I said, and walked home full of the same dread I'd felt the first time Moe Nagic took me into the world of the old brudge.

"Nick," said Mum after we kissed hello, "are you all right? You don't quite look yourself."

"I'm OK," I said, "really." By then the dread was ringing in me like a telephone and I knew I was wanted on the old brudge. It was no longer a matter of choice –

it was the next thing in my life and I had to get to it. I went up to my room and started my Maths prep; I would have gone to the juzzle world straightaway but I couldn't take a chance on what kind of shape I'd be in when I got back.

It seemed no more than five minutes later, when I was doing my Maths prep, that Dad knocked on my door and came in. When he saw the put-together juzzle he knelt down and had a close look at it for a while. "It's obviously twentieth century," he said, "but the mood reminds me of Thomas Girtin a little."

"Who's Thomas Girtin?"

"Late eighteenth, early nineteenth-century water-colourist. We've got a little book from the Tate with a couple of his pictures in it."

"I didn't know you were interested in watercolours."

"There might even be one or two other things you don't know about me." He gave me a look that I understand better now than I did then: he wanted to be recognised as someone in his own right, not just as my father. "This picture, though," he said. "I don't especially like it."

"Why not?"

"I don't know – there's something depressing about it."

"Do you really think so?"

"Yes, I do. And speaking of depression, are you feeling a bit down at the moment?"

"No, I feel the same as always."

"Because, you know, if you *are* feeling down and you need to talk about anything, I'm here and I might be able to help with whatever's on your mind."

I DOUBT IT, said my mind.

"I know you doubt it," said Dad, "but you might possibly be wrong. You're just approaching puberty or maybe you've reached it already, and that can be a confusing time. We've never talked about that sort of thing and maybe now we should."

"Thanks, Dad, but right now the only thing on my mind is my Maths prep."

He heaved a big sigh, of relief I thought. "Right. Just remember that I'm there if you need me."

"I will, Dad." I was feeling guilty because I didn't want him getting into the juzzle thing. The one I needed was Moe Nagic.

WHAT DO YOU NEED HIM FOR? said my mind.

Well, there are a lot of things I want to ask him about.

HE'S ALREADY TOLD YOU ALL YOU NEED TO KNOW. WHAT ARE YOU LOOKING FOR – MAGIC PASSWORDS, A CLOAK OF INVISIBILITY, WINGED SANDALS? WHAT?

Never mind – I can see this isn't something you and I can talk about.

IT ISN'T SOMETHING YOU AND ANYONE CAN TALK ABOUT. YOU'VE JUST GOT TO DO IT.

All right. Thanks very much for your support. I'll be in touch.

I got through my prep, through dinner and flute practice, and then I was alone with the juzzle again. I spun the gyroscope, leaned into the picture when it said WAY IN, drowned in blackness, found myself on the brudge, and put the gyroscope where it was safe. This time the light was different: instead of the thundery twilight there was a bright fog; from where I stood in the middle of the brudge I couldn't see either end.

I thought I heard music – very, very faintly. I had to listen hard to pull it out of the silence. It was '*Libertango*' of course, played on a concertina as I'd heard Moe Nagic do it. I imagined him and Zelda in the spotlight when he made Zelda disappear, then I pictured him lying in the street when Zelda disappeared with Charles.

The fog became a stagy darkness with a white spotlight and there was Moe Nagic in white tie and tails and young again. With a flourish he took off his top hat, put his hand into it, and brought it out again, empty. Then he and the brudge and everything else disappeared and I drowned in blackness and was back in my room.

It took me a long time to get to sleep that night; I kept seeing Moe Nagic on the brudge pulling nothing out of his hat.

4

Glimmers

The next day was Wednesday, two days after my encounter with Moe Nagic in the Castleford Road. School normal, no action on the Buncher front. Tom Jeffreys asked me over to play chess after school and I was glad to have something to distract me from my thoughts about Moe Nagic. I kept seeing him reach into that top hat and pull out nothing.

What do you think he was trying to tell me? I said to my mind.

DO YOU REALLY NEED TO ASK ME?

I guess not.

HAVE YOU NEVER REACHED INTO THE HAT AND PULLED OUT NOTHING?

The last History test, I suppose.

GO ON.

Those three fights with Buncher, right?

GO ON.

And the first two times I went to the old brudge alone?

YOU SAID IT, I DIDN'T.

All right, I'll try to do better.

"Your move," said Tom.

"Later," I said. "This evening."

"What are you talking about? This isn't postal chess – I've just put you in check with my knight and you've got to do something about it now."

"Sorry." I moved my king and Tom took my rook.

"You haven't got your mind on the game," he said. "You don't usually let me get you in a fork like that."

"Not my day, I guess." From the next room came the sound of a piano, the beginning of something over and over with stops and starts. It had the same flavour as '*Claire de Lune*'.

"Cynthia," said Tom. "Practising her new piece."

"Is it Debussy?"

"I don't know." He shouted, "Hey, Cyn!"

"What?" came her answer.

"What's that you're trying to play?"

She came into the room then. Every time I saw her she seemed more beautiful. " '*Reverie*'," she said, "by Debussy."

"I *thought* it must be Debussy," I said. "My mother's always playing '*Clair de Lune*'."

"That reminds me," she said, "you were in a dream I had the other night."

Cynthia Jeffreys dreaming about me! My heart began to pound so hard that I thought she must be hearing it but she gave no sign. "What was the dream?"

"All I can remember is that I was in amongst some trees and there was a dark sky, all thundery. And I saw you on a bridge. I've no idea what you were doing there or what I was doing in the wood but there was a feeling of danger. I think I woke up then – at least that's all I can remember."

I almost fell out of my chair. Cynthia Jeffreys dreaming

42

herself into the juzzle world with me! Cynthia in danger! It was too much for me to take in, I had to give myself time to think about it. "I'd never let any harm come to you," I blurted out. Then I realised how ridiculous that must sound to her. I mean, as far as she knew it was her dream, so how could I have anything to say about what I'd do or not do?

But Cynthia didn't laugh. She gave me a look that made me weak in the knees. "I know you wouldn't, Nick," she said.

"I don't think I've got any more chess in me today," I said to Tom. "You've got that game well and truly won so I'll resign."

"I think you might have done better if you'd paid a little more attention to what you were doing," said Tom.

"You're right. I'll try to do better next time." I almost said, 'See you in your dreams' to Cynthia but decided not to – it sounded so sleazy compared to the way I felt. "See you," I said.

On my way out I almost bumped into Mrs Jeffreys. She was standing in the hall with her back to me, reading a newspaper and humming 'Libertango'. "Was I humming that when we were playing chess?" I said to her.

She turned towards me and for a moment I could see Cynthia in her face. "What?" she said.

"That tune – did you hear me humming it a little while ago?"

"I don't know. Sometimes a tune is just in the air. See you, Nick," and she drifted upstairs.

Walking down Castleford Road I passed a newsagent. *The Castleford Chronicle* comes out on Wednesdays and there was a stack of it on the rack. Smiling up at me from the front page were Moe Nagic and Zelda in the photograph I'd seen in the old handbill he showed me. THE NAGIC IS GONE, said the headline over the picture, putting into words what I hadn't wanted to think when I saw him on the brudge the night before. We'd have the paper at home and I wanted to be alone with that news so I hurried on, looking away from Moe Nagic's empty pitch when I passed it.

At home I kissed Mum hello, grabbed *The Castleford Chronicle* off the umbrella stand in the hall, took it up to my room, and read the caption under the photo and the story that followed:

> Morris Nagic and Zelda Watson as they appeared on Brighton Pier in the 70s.

> Morris Nagic, 47, was found dead in his flat in the Harrington Estate by a neighbour yesterday. An empty bottle of sleeping tablets and a note were on a bedside table. Nagic, although never a big name in 'showbiz', was in his time a popular entertainer on the seaside circuit with his magic act. After breaking up with his partner Zelda Watson in 1977 he gave up magic and was until recently a postal clerk. Diagnosed as having terminal cancer early this year, he resigned from his job and spent most of his remaining time in the streets, busking with a concertina.

Moe Nagic smiled out at me from the photograph but his eyes weren't smiling. He was staring as if entranced, and when I covered up the smile his eyes seemed very large, full of terror and mystery. I had the feeling that his eyes were telling me something that I already knew but had forgotten. Looking at Zelda I felt a sudden rush of sadness; I think that was the first time it hit me that everybody grows old and dies. Moe Nagic was gone and Zelda must be in her forties by now, not young and beautiful as she was in the photograph. Even Cynthia would grow old and I too, and one day there'd be no more us. I looked out of my window at the chestnut tree that stood there in the late afternoon sunlight and shook my head.

Mum was calling me from downstairs. I went to the landing and shouted, "What?"

"There's a policeman here to see you," she said.

"A policeman!" I went down and there he was in the front hall looking up at me while Mum hovered anxiously nearby.

"Nick, this is Police Constable Rutherford," she said. "Apparently he needs to ask you some questions."

"Did you know Morris Nagic?" said PC Rutherford.

"Yes."

"Did you know he was found dead yesterday?"

"Yes, I was just reading about it in *The Chronicle*."

"Have you looked at the *Personal* columns?"

"No."

"If you had you might have seen this." He handed me a note. There was a telephone number and under it, in very shaky handwriting:

> *Enquiries about a watercolour painting,* THE
> OLD BRUDGE, *should be addressed to its
> present owner, Nick Hartley, 12, Tinker's Lane,
> Richmond.*

45

"Is this the note that was mentioned in the paper?" I said.

"That's it. The telephone number is for *Chronicle* Classified. He placed that ad by phone on the afternoon he took the overdose. Any idea what it's about?"

"Moe Nagic sold me that painting and a gyroscope for two pounds forty-two but I don't know why there should be any enquiries."

"When was this?"

"Day before yesterday – Monday."

"How'd you come to buy the picture?"

"He was sitting on the pavement near The Green Man and he had some things to sell and we got to talking and I bought the picture and the gyroscope. The picture was cut up into a jigsaw puzzle."

"Could I see this puzzle?"

"Sure." I took him up to my room and showed him the juzzle. I'd moved it into its box and it looked exactly as it had looked when I bought it from Moe Nagic. Mum had followed us and was standing by.

"Is Nick in any sort of trouble?" she said.

"None at all," said PC Rutherford. "This is simply the routine follow-up we do in situations like this. Mind if I look at the back of the puzzle?" he asked me.

"No, go ahead."

He took the lid, put it on the box, then held it shut while he turned the whole thing over and lifted the box off the juzzle. The backing was cardboard and there was nothing written on it or stuck to it. He put the box back on to the juzzle and turned it over so that it faced up again when he took off the lid. He picked at the edge of

46

the juzzle to see if the paper could be peeled away from the backing.

"Don't do that," I said, "you'll spoil my juzzle."

"Juzzle?"

"Puzzle."

"I don't think you're allowed to do that without a warrant," said Mum to PC Rutherford.

"Sorry," he said, and stopped. "I'm just wondering if there's any writing on the back."

"And if there is?" said Mum. "Suppose the artist signed it on the back, what then? Is there any sort of crime connected with this picture? What are you looking for?"

"I don't know. I can't help being curious about his note, you see – it makes one wonder whether the boy is being used as some sort of message drop."

"I think you've been watching too many spy films," said Mum. "Had Morris Nagic a criminal record?"

"Not that we know of."

"Well then," said Mum. "There's no reason for you to be suspicious, is there?"

"None that I know at the present time. However, if there should be enquiries about this picture that you find worrying in any way, please let us know."

"Of course."

"Right," said PC Rutherford. "That's it then. Here's a number for you to call." He gave Mum a card and off he went.

"Nick," said Mum. "What was that all about?"

"I've absolutely no idea," I said.

"How well did you know this Morris Nagic?"

"I talked to him for about twenty minutes and I

bought the puzzle and the gyroscope from him – that's it."

"You're sure there was nothing more?"

"Mum, he did not offer me sweets and take me to his place, if that's the sort of thing you're worrying about. All that happened is exactly what I've told you and the PC."

"In any case he seems to have taken a liking to you."

"I don't know. If he topped himself shortly after that there's no telling what his state of mind was."

"Who knows? Maybe one day a solicitor will ring us up and say that Morris Nagic has left you pots of money."

"He didn't look as if he had pots of money."

"They often don't, then they turn out to have a fortune that they leave to a cat cemetery or a masseuse or whatever."

When Dad came home he got into it as well with more questions and speculations of his own. A drug ring was his favourite theory, and he warned us all to be on the lookout for suspicious cars or loiterers. David of course had one or two things to say about what he called Dad's xenophobia and they kicked that around for a while. Dad also said that it wouldn't be a bad idea to peel the picture off its backing to see if there was anything on the other side but I refused to allow that.

Everything seemed to be expanding and requiring more space than I had in me and I needed more and more time to think about it all. I'd never had death come so close to me and my thoughts kept going to it the way your tongue goes into a cavity. When I'd seen Moe Nagic on the brudge I'd felt that was his goodbye but I hadn't

48

wanted to believe it. Reading of his death the next day while I was still trying to get my head around Cynthia's dream – it was all a little too much for me. The note he'd left seemed to be pulling me further into Moe Nagic's life and binding me to him. It's embarrassing to say this but I'd rated him as a loser and I didn't want to be sucked into the vortex he made when he sank. I know that earlier in these pages I wrote that I knew we were in this thing together but now I wished we weren't. Plus I didn't want any new people coming into my life with enquiries about the watercolour – whoever they were and whatever they wanted could only add to the burden I was already carrying. I'd soldier on because I couldn't help wanting to know how it would come out but I wasn't enjoying it.

That evening I put off doing the juzzle until we'd said our goodnights because I didn't want to have to talk to anyone when I got back from the world of the old brudge. The room was dark but with the curtains open there was enough light from the street lamps for me to see what I was doing. I gave the string a good pull, and when I knew the flywheel was saying WAY IN I leant into the picture, did my drowning, and found myself again on the old brudge.

I put the gyroscope in its safe place on the paving, then with my eyes on the little would I moved forward. A silence sprang up around me; I could feel it pressing on my face in the twilight. Then I heard from far away the music of Debussy's '*Reverie*', just the beginning of it, haltingly, over and over. In that little clump of trees on the hill I saw a glimmer of something, a white dress moving through the dimness. It was Cynthia Jeffreys, even at that distance I recognised her. Was she in danger? What was she doing in this place? I was about to run towards her when a figure loomed up in front of me. He had his back towards me but there was no mistaking Buncher. He turned and this time I heard him when he spoke. "I saw her first," he said.

He came at me with a rush but I sidestepped and he went past me. I heard something crunch and I knew what had happened. When I turned to face him again I saw the smashed gyroscope and I thought my heart would jump out of my body.

Will I be able to get back? I said to my mind as Buncher came at me in slow motion; it was like a moment that would never go away.

BACK WHERE? said my mind.

As Buncher came towards me I went in low, grabbed his legs, and using his momentum, twisted to the left, heaved up and back as hard as I could, and sent him flying over my shoulder, over the parapet and into whatever flowed beneath the brudge.

Please tell me, I said to my mind as I ran across the bridge towards the hill and the little would, am I going to be able to get home all right?

THIS IS HOME, it said.

No, it isn't. This is some other reality and you're making it happen. The gyroscope was just to get you focused on this, it wasn't magic or anything, right? There's no magic and as soon as I find Cynthia and get this sorted we're going home, OK?

THIS IS HOME.

5

The Little Would

My mind couldn't have meant that, I told myself. It knows this isn't home and after a while this place will disappear because I'm not really here, I'm in my room in our house. I just have to see what's happening with Cynthia and that'll probably be as much as I can do this trip. Then I'll go to bed.

Up the hill I went, seeing every blade of grass and every pebble very clearly. Then I was in among the trees where the air seemed made of shadows and the spaces were all twisty. The trees were all somehow crippled-looking, wrong in their shapes. The ground was littered with dead leaves and fallen branches and all kinds of rubbish: rusty tin cans, a rotting car seat, used condoms, crumpled empty cigarette packets, a broken suitcase full of pulpy letters with rain-blurred handwriting, a lady's shoe and soggy newspapers from years ago.

Moe Nagic had made it clear to me that this was a mind trip so I knew that my mind was showing me whatever I saw. Where was it getting its material from? The old brudge and the little would could be seen in the watercolour so obviously they'd come from the painter's viewing of some real or imagined place. Moe Nagic had seen the mise and Trokeville and he'd told me I'd find them in the juzzle world so those had to be set items on the menu regardless of whose mind made them happen. But probably each item was different for everyone and Moe Nagic's little would hadn't been the same as mine. And the painter – what sort of little would had *he* had? His maze or mise, what might that have been, and had he done the troke and got to Trokeville?

I picked up a handful of rain-sodden letters from the suitcase and went through them until I came to one more legible than the others. The date was from twenty-two years ago and I read:

> Dearest Violet,
>
> Sometimes when I open one of your letters and smell your scent on the paper and see the words formed by your hand I can't believe it, can't believe that you actually love me. I don't know how it happened that out of all the people in the world we found each other. Sometimes I'm afraid that I'll wake up and find that it was all a dream.

Violet is my mother's name. I stopped reading and put the letter back with the others. Maybe the Violet the letter was written to was a different Violet – I didn't want to look any further to see if the letters were signed with Dad's name or someone else's. Reading that bit of the letter I could see a young man writing it, deeply in love and aching to be with his Violet. Mum is still a good-looking woman at her age and of course she's lovable but until then I'd never thought of her as a recipient of love letters.

After reading that letter it took me a few moments to remember where I was and why I was there, then it came back to me: the glimmer of white, the distant figure of Cynthia Jeffreys moving through the little would, and Harry Buncher coming at me. And I'd thrown him into that stinking black river! He wouldn't half be mad now. Mustn't think of that. Where was Cynthia? I walked and walked, for hours it seemed and always uphill. I was sure that I ought to be going down the other side of that hill by now. The little would hadn't looked all that big but there seemed to be no end to it. The twilight was darkening into night, the shadows clung to me like cobwebs and the spaces kept shifting. I wanted to keep moving but I'd no idea which way to go – I couldn't even be sure I was walking straight ahead. For all I knew I was going in circles, so I stopped and tried to think what to do next.

THIS IS THE LITTLE WOULD, said my mind.

I know that, and I'm lost in it.

A LITTLE WOULD ISN'T ENOUGH.

What do you mean?

THINK ABOUT IT.

If a little would isn't enough, what then? A more than little would? A big would?

TRY THAT.

I tried to sense where the little would in me was coming from. It seemed to be somewhere around my solar plexus, so I closed my eyes and did my best to send my self, the self of me, down there to more than little would. Easier said than done. I strained until I thought my guts would burst but I wasn't getting my self where I wanted it to be. It seemed a long time since I'd seen the glimmer of white that was Cynthia; the air was like wet flannel on my face; the trees seemed to be moving in on me and the spaces between them were rubbing against me like cats. Everything was slowing me down and I was certain that Buncher was out of the river by now and hot on my trail. "Oh shit!" I said. "I'll never get out of here!"

LITTLE WOULD I HAVE THOUGHT YOU WERE SUCH A WANKER, said my mind.

"All right," I said aloud to myself, not caring who or what heard me, "time to pull yourself together. This must be like when you get into trouble swimming. Mustn't panic. Turn over on your back and float while you calm down." So I mentally turned over on my back and floated until I calmed down. Then I willed my self down to where I was little woulding. My fear was down there so I tried to let the rest of me join up with it. That worked and immediately I felt twice as scared; the trees got bigger and darker and more misshapen and I could hear a deep grinding sound as if their roots were walking down under the ground while the trunks and branches crowded me. The spaces were coiling themselves around me like snakes.

"*Big* would," I said. "I'm doing a big would now so you better back off." I could feel my self humping itself up. I was growling a little and there was a smell that I seemed to remember as if from another life, a life when rage came easily. It felt good. "You want bother?" I said. "I'll *give* you bother!" I didn't know how I was going to manage that but the trees and the spaces seemed to move back a little and I could see a bit better. Looking behind me I saw Buncher coming up the hill. Looking ahead I thought I saw the glimmer of white again. Off to my right there was another figure moving through the trees and that annoyed me; it was hard enough keeping up with things from moment to moment without having to pay attention to new players.

The air seemed to have thinned out a bit and I began to think that I more than little would find a way out of where I was. I was getting a sense of the direction in which Cynthia had gone so I headed that way. 'Libert-ango' was singing itself in my head:

> Strange – I've seen that face before,
> seen him hanging round my door,
> like a hawk feeling for the prey,
> like a night waiting for the day.

There was much more space between the trees now and I had a better view of the figure to my right – it was a man running in the same direction I was. I couldn't see his face but there was something familiar about the general look of him. Then he turned towards me and it was Dad. I couldn't believe it. "What are *you* doing here?" I shouted.

"What am *I* doing here?" he shouted back. "I've been trying to find a way out of here for years. Why are you here?"

"It's a long story, Dad."

"It'll have to wait then – can't talk now, I'm trying to catch up with your mother."

"What's Mum here for?"

"I don't know and I'm worried about her. Help me find her – she's somewhere up ahead."

I tried to get over to where he was but some trees came between us and I lost sight of him.

"Can you hear me, Nick?" His voice came to me from farther away than before.

"Just barely."

"Don't *you* get stuck here. Don't let anything stop you from . . ." I couldn't make out the rest of it.

"From what? I didn't catch that last bit."

". . . wanted to be . . ." came his words from even farther away.

"What, Dad? What did you want to be?" But I got no answer to that. When I came into the clear he was nowhere to be seen so I just kept on running straight ahead, wondering if the glimmer of white had been Mum and not Cynthia. I was thinking about Dad too but not all that much. I didn't like finding my parents in this place; whatever it was, I wanted it to be mine and nothing to do with my family. Just as I had that thought I almost ran into David. He was sitting on the ground with his back against a tree, looking completely relaxed.

"Why aren't you running?" I said.

"And I could ask you why you are," he answered.

"I'm trying to find Cynthia Jeffreys, Mum too. Dad's here looking for her as well."

"Good luck with finding Cynthia, Nick, but there's nothing you can do for Mum and Dad – they've been stuck here for a long time and they're going to have to find their own way out. Or not. I'm not running because I'm not buying into this illusion, OK? If it works for you, fine, but it's nothing to do with me so I'll see you later." He got up and stepped behind a tree and then he wasn't there any more.

While I'd been running through the little would the twilight had become proper night but nothing like night at home: you couldn't see your hand in front of your face. I'd once read a story, *Witch Wood* by Lord Dunsany, about a little hazel wood, just a clump of trees that was no problem to get through in the daytime but it had been cursed by a witch and if you went into it at night you'd be hopelessly lost until the dawn. I hoped I wasn't going to have to be here any longer than that. The owls were calling again and I could hear someone not too far behind me, probably Buncher. Listen, I said to my mind, could we knock off now and come back here tomorrow? It's too dark to see anything, I'm very tired, and I'd like to go home and get some rest so I can be fresh for whatever comes after this part.

ARE YOU STUPID OR WHAT? said my mind. I KEEP TELLING YOU, THIS *IS* HOME. I'M STUCK IN THIS MODE AND I DON'T KNOW ANYTHING ELSE UNTIL YOU GET US THROUGH IT. YOU WANT ME TO PUT IT MORE SIMPLY THAN THAT? ACTION TALKS, BULLSHIT WALKS, OK?

You never used to speak to me that way.

GET US OUT OF THIS LITTLE WOULD AND MAYBE I'LL BE NICE TO YOU AGAIN.

There was a really awful smell coming towards me – it was the smell of that black river. "Nick?" said a voice out of the dark. I almost jumped out of my skin. "It's me, Harry Buncher."

"Don't I know it! You smell even worse than usual."

"Do I? Maybe next time I'll throw *you* into that river, see how *you* smell then."

It was strange, talking to my old enemy in the dark like that. Not being able to see his face made me feel much freer and the fact of my having thrown him into the river was a big help too. "We'll see about next time next time," I said. "What's on your mind?"

"How come I'm here? Is this a dream or what?"

"I don't know what it is for you. It's not a dream for me – it's a special kind of reality."

"I bet it is, too – what with Cynthia Jeffreys in it. *She's* a very special bit of reality, eh?"

"Careful! You might end up in the river again."

"You got lucky once but you won't do that twice, Nicky. Right now what I'd like to know is how do I get out of this special reality of yours?"

"I don't know what to tell you, Harry. Maybe you'll wake up or tune out or something. Me, I'm stuck here until I get through it."

"Through what, though? What's all this about?"

"I'm not really sure. When it started I thought it was just about one or two things but now I'm beginning to think it's about everything."

"I don't like it. Is this your way of getting back at me for heading you the other day?"

"I honestly don't know what it is and I don't want to think about it any more tonight – I just want to get some rest so I'm in some kind of shape for tomorrow."

"You think we'll still be here tomorrow?"

"I told you, Harry, I don't know about you but I'm stuck here until I work my way out."

"Yeah, but why'd you have to drag me into it?"

Had I dragged him into it? I was trying to remember how it all started: the fight with Buncher and having my head banged into the wall; walking home along the Castleford Road with my head feeling strange; meeting Moe Nagic; hearing his long story about him and Zelda and his fight with Charles and how he got into the picture of the old bridge and so on. There'd been some talk of winning and losing, there'd been talk of all kinds of things but I'd never mentioned Harry Buncher.

EXCUSE ME, said my mind.

What?

I WAS JUST TRYING TO REMEMBER HOW IT HAPPENED THAT YOU BOUGHT THAT JUZZLE AND THE GYROSCOPE FROM MOE NAGIC.

Well, you know, I saw the thing and we got to talking and he told me about what happened to him . . .

HE TOLD YOU HOW HE LOST A FIGHT AND ZELDA WENT OFF WITH CHARLES.

That's right.

AND YOU'D JUST LOST A FIGHT YOURSELF THAT DAY.

Yes, I had.

AND MOE NAGIC TOLD YOU TO THINK WINNING.

Yes, he did.

THEN HE TOOK YOU INTO THE PICTURE OF THE OLD BRIDGE.

Brudge.

BRUDGE. HE TOOK YOU INTO THAT OTHER REALITY WHERE TROKEVILLE IS.

So?

AND YOU BOUGHT THAT JUZZLE AND TOOK IT HOME SO YOU COULD GET INTO THAT OTHER REALITY.

Yes.

TO DO WHAT?

Do better, I guess.

DO BETTER AGAINST HARRY BUNCHER, YES?

All right, yes.

SO WHY DON'T YOU GIVE HARRY BUNCHER A STRAIGHT ANSWER?

"Harry," I said, "what was your question again?"

"What're you, deaf? I said why'd you have to drag me into this?"

"I didn't drag you into it, stupid. This is my reality, and you jumped into it when you started giving me bother."

"Who are you calling stupid?"

"You, I think. It's hard to be sure in the dark."

"You're getting pretty free with your mouth, Nicky boy."

"I speak as I find, Harry boy."

"If it wasn't so dark I'd teach you a lesson right now."

"Somehow I don't see you as a teacher."

"You will, though, believe me."

"I'll work on it. Now can we go to sleep?"

"Sleep! I'm cold and wet – I'm only wearing pyjamas and I've got this black shit from the river all over me."

"Well, try not to fall in next time."

"I'll make you sorry for this, Nick."

"I don't think you can, Harry."

"We'll see about that."

"I expect we shall. Now it's good night from me. See you in the morning."

"You can count on that."

So there we were, the two of us getting ready to spend a night in this little would in my mind. Weird! Although there was a thick layer of dead leaves on the ground and there ought to have been a reasonably soft place to lie down, wherever I put myself there seemed to be hard things sticking into me. We both kicked rubbish and fallen branches out of the way and trampled out places not too close to each other. Then we lay down in the damp and the dank smell of rotting leaves and rubbish but despite my tiredness I couldn't fall asleep. Behind my closed eyes I saw the white glimmer of Cynthia, then the blue Pacific from my high peak, then came thoughts of Mum and Dad. When I'd seen Dad through the trees he'd looked younger, less grown-up than he usually did. Maybe, I thought suddenly, nobody ever grows up – they just get old and die. And Mum, with her not-quite-together playing of 'Claire de Lune', maybe there was a lot I didn't know about her. Here she was in this little would, running away from something or running towards something? Oh God, I said to my mind. I've got more on my plate than I can deal with.

WELCOME TO LIFE.

After a long time I fell asleep and dreamt of fighting with shadows, heavy ones that smelt bad. The shadows were winning and I woke up with my heart beating fast, then fell back into the same dream. I don't know how many times I did that but I think the final score must have been something like SHADOWS 6 NICK 0.

Strange! Really strange, falling asleep and waking up in the little would and knowing all the time that I was actually in my room at home bent over a homemade jigsaw puzzle. I'd no idea what the time was in the regular world; for all I knew the events of last night had happened in less than a minute, the way they do in dreams; or maybe it really was the next day and I was meant to be in school.

The morning light in the little would was dark and dim and the ugly trees with their ugly in-between spaces looked desolate. The whole scene had a cheapo feel to it, like a not very good film made on a very low budget. I was only wearing pyjamas the same as Harry Buncher, and after a night on the ground in that place I was chilled to the bone and aching all over.

And there was Buncher in that miserable morning light, big as life and twice as smelly with that black muck all over him. He was coughing in quite a serious way. "I think I might've got pneumonia," he said.

"That makes two of us." We both stood around coughing and shivering for a while, then went and did our separate pees and came back and stood looking at each other. The night before, in the dark, I'd been on a high from throwing Buncher into the river and I realised that I might have let my mouth run away with me a little. Now he was giving me a hard look with that evil face of his and I wasn't quite so sure of myself as I had been. I thought he might be about to come at me at any moment so I got ready.

"What, are you looking for another beating?" he said.

"Whatever, Harry."

"Look, right now I think my first priority is to get out of this. What say we declare a truce until we're back in the real world?"

"As long as you don't try anything on with Cynthia if we find her."

"You're talking very tough for a guy who loses all his fights, Nicky."

"I didn't lose the one on the brudge, did I."

"You mean bridge. I told you, you just got lucky that time."

"Don't change the subject, Harry. Keep away from Cynthia or no truce."

"Nicky boy, I think you might be getting a little ahead of yourself. Are you really ready for Cynthia Jeffreys? Are you up for that kind of action?"

I could feel my face going red and Buncher let out a big guffaw. "I don't believe you are," he said. "I bet you haven't even had your first wet dream yet, have you?"

I hadn't. In the showers after games at school I couldn't help noticing that some of the other boys of my age had more pubic hair and were more developed than I was. Buncher, at thirteen, with his hormones and his pong, looked pretty much like a man already. "You just keep away from Cynthia," I said.

"Dog in the manger sort of thing?" said Buncher. "You can't do it so you don't want anybody else to? I've had some experience, you know." His hand went to his crotch in case I'd missed the point. "I could show Cynthia a really good time and have her begging for more. She's got a lovely arse, that girl. Oh, yes, she . . ."

That was when I hit him in the face as hard as I could but it wasn't hard enough. "You little bastard!" he yelled, and threw himself at me. I was knocked off my feet and then I was on my back and he was sitting on me with his hands on my throat. This was no schoolboy fight any more – he was trying to strangle me. I gave him a hard chop in the throat and as he loosened his grip I rolled sideways on to something hard. I felt for it with my right hand – an old rusty shovel with the handle broken off short. I got a good grip on it but by this time Buncher was on his feet and aiming a kick at my head. I grabbed his foot with my free hand and brought him crashing down. Then I swung that old rusty shovel and caught him on the side of the head with the flat of it. There was some blood and he didn't move. My senses seemed sharper than they ordinarily were – I thought I could smell the blood and I liked that smell.

WELL, YOU SURE AS HELL WON THAT ONE, said my mind.

I haven't killed him, have I? Moe Nagic said this was a mind trip – Buncher's not really hurt in the regular world, is he?

I DON'T KNOW ABOUT THE REGULAR WORLD ANY MORE.

But what should I do with him?

LEAVE HIM HERE FOR ALL I CARE.

I don't think I can do that; I don't think I'd want that done to me.

PLEASE YOURSELF THEN.

There was poor old Buncher out cold with a lump on the side of his head about the size of the one I'd had when he headed me into the wall. All pale and still like that he didn't seem as ugly as usual. I felt for his pulse and I was relieved to find one – I didn't want him to be dead. That is, I wouldn't have minded his being dead but I didn't want to be the one who'd killed him. I'd no idea how to bring him round; I slapped his face a couple of times without any result. I didn't really want to do mouth-to-mouth but I felt that I had to try something so I did it: nothing.

I managed to get him over my shoulder in the fire-man's carry, and not knowing what else to do I staggered back down the hill with him and headed towards where I thought the brudge was. The spaces between the trees seemed to open up for me and in a little while I could see the brudge. On the far side of it, where a viewer of the scene in *The Old Brudge* watercolour would have stood, there was someone sitting on a folding stool doing a watercolour. I noticed that the sky had got darker – now it was that eerie twilight you get just before a storm. The leaves of the trees were pattering and showing their undersides and there were flickers of lightning and rum-blings of thunder. You think of everything, don't you, I said to my mind.

THIS IS WHERE I AM, THIS IS WHAT THERE IS.

Do you think that man might have a car nearby and he could take Buncher to the nearest hospital?

I DON'T KNOW. ASK HIM.

The brudge was between me and the watercolour painter but because I was on high ground we could both see each other clearly. Strange, I thought as I got closer to him, I've seen that face before. He seemed angry as he worked and was completely absorbed in his painting but then he paused, dabbled his brush in the water can, flicked the water off it, and leant back for a look at what he'd done. He must have seen me and he must have noticed that I was pretty well exhausted from carrying Buncher but he didn't come to help me, just went on painting. He was on the same side of the river as I, so I reached him in a few minutes. "Moe Nagic?" I said, because for a moment that's who I thought it was.

"No," he said, "there isn't."

"Sorry, I thought you were someone else."

"I've sometimes thought that but it doesn't really change anything." He wasn't all that much like Moe Nagic, now that I had a closer look. It was just an average sort of face that at a quick glance could have been anyone you wanted it to be. He was wearing the sort of little white hat with a floppy brim that you see at the seaside, a white T-shirt, a very old pair of jeans, and tennis shoes. His face was shaded by the hat but apart from that it seemed shadowy in itself.

I offloaded Buncher on to the ground as gently as I could. There was quite a bit of blood from where I'd hit him with the shovel. He groaned a little but didn't open his eyes and he still looked very pale. "He needs help," I said to the painter.

"So many of us do," he said, and went on painting.

"Have you got a car?"

"Yes." When he spoke his lips didn't seem to be forming the words that I heard – it was a bit like those foreign films with English dubbed on to them.

"Could you take him to the nearest hospital, please? He really ought to be seen by a doctor, I think."

"All right." But he went on painting. The stench of the river was very strong and the wind was blowing it towards us.

"Doesn't the smell of that river bother you?" I said.

"No more than anything else." He stopped painting and leant the watercolour block against a rock. I came round for a better look. It was the picture I was in, the picture that Moe Nagic had cut up into a jigsaw. He rinsed his brush in the water can, flicked the water off it, put it in his paintbox, closed the box, and folded up his stool.

"Aren't you going to sign it?" I said.

"What for? I'm nobody."

I had another look at the brudge: nobody on it. "Who are the two people on the brudge in your picture?" I said.

"They're whoever happens to come along next. I just put them in to add a little boredom to the scene."

"Why would you want to add boredom to it?"

"Everything else hurts too much." He picked up the watercolour block and the rest of his gear and started up the bank. I had just enough strength left to put Buncher over my shoulder again and carry him to where the car was, on a bit of road I hadn't noticed before. The car was a Morris Minor Traveller. The painter opened up the rear and left it to me to get Buncher inside while he put his things into the front seat. As he got in and started up the car I said, "Thanks very much for your help. The boy in the back is Harry Buncher and I'm Nick Hartley."

"Whatever you like," he said, and drove away.

Well, I said to my mind, that's Buncher out of the picture for a while at least. Actually, we could have used a little more detail in that bit. Who was that man?

NO IDEA.

I'd like to know more about him and I'd like to have asked him how the painting ended up in Mrs Whitby's Seaview Hotel.

WHAT THERE WAS IS ALL THERE WAS. I CAN'T DO MORE THAN THAT. THE LITTLE WOULD, YOU'VE STILL GOT IT TO DO.

You're making this up as you go along, aren't you?

THIS IS WHERE I AM, THIS IS WHAT THERE IS.

You said that before. Where does the painter come into it, though? Is he just an extra you brought in to get Harry Buncher out of here or has he got some deeper meaning?

NOBODY TELLS ME ANYTHING. ALL I KNOW IS WHAT HAPPENS – PEOPLE COME INTO IT AND PEOPLE GO OUT OF IT AND THIS IS WHAT THERE IS.

I turned and looked uphill towards the little would. The trees and the spaces looked pretty much the same as before and again I caught that glimmer of a white dress through the trees. I made a megaphone of my hands and shouted, "Cynthia! Is that you?"

No answer, and the white dress was gone. I started up that hill again, through the dead leaves, the soggy newspapers and used condoms and the rest of the rubbish. The sky was absolutely black and there came a crash of thunder and a bolt of lightning that half-blinded me and split a tree only a few metres in front of me, close enough for me to smell the electricity and the burnt wood. I wondered if it was possible to be killed by lightning on a mind trip. Then came a downpour that soaked me to the skin and I wondered about mind-trip pneumonia. By now I was thoroughly into it; I wasn't worrying about school or parents or anything else – I accepted that this was where I was and this was what I was doing; this was my world now.

There was another crash of thunder and in the lightning flash I saw the white dress again. "Cynthia?" I shouted.

"Who's there?" came the answer, not in Cynthia's voice. Whoever it was sounded frightened.

"Nick Hartley," I said. "Who are you?"

"Zelda Watson." There was another flash of lightning and this time I saw her clearly only a few feet away. For a moment I thought it was Cynthia, she looked so much like her, so young and beautiful, more beautiful than in the photograph. "This place – " she said. "I didn't mean to be here but it keeps coming back."

"You've been here before? You've been over the old brudge?"

"Oh God – so many times. Why are you here?"

"Moe Nagic . . ." I said, then I reminded myself that this was the Zelda of twenty-odd years ago so she couldn't know that Moe Nagic was dead. I wasn't sure what to tell her if she asked me about him but all she said was, "Oh." I took her hand and, not knowing what gave me the right to do that, said, "Let's see if we can find some place where we can get out of the rain." She was much more beautiful than the Zelda in the photograph; the touch of her hand was thrilling – I seemed to feel in it the life she'd had with Moe Nagic, whatever happiness there'd been and the sadness of their parting. And yet, even though her hand was warm in mine and her dress was wet with real rain and there were real drops of water in her hair and running down her face, she seemed to be someone who couldn't be held and might disappear at any moment.

There was no shelter anywhere but the rain eased off and stopped and the thunder got more distant and the sky lightened up. We stopped to rest for a bit and she looked at me as if she was waiting for the questions I was about to ask. I didn't want to confuse things by knowing more than she'd expect me to so I waited for her to speak.

"I've left Moe Nagic," she said.

"Oh."

"It's so hard to know if you're doing the right thing."

"I know."

"You don't want to be cruel to anyone but sometimes life is cruel."

"Yes, it is."

"Nick, how old are you?"

"Almost thirteen."

"Do you want there to be magic?"

"Yes, I do."

She squeezed my hand. "For a while when I was with Moe the world was like a great big glitterball, turning and changing and the scatterings of light moving over the dancers in the dark. The band always played a tango for the disappearing act . . ." She hummed the opening bars of 'Libertango'. "There was magic in that music, it kept moving forward and holding back at the same time – it was like the sand being sucked out from under your feet when you stand at the water's edge – and that shadowy theme snaking in on the synthesiser. 'Come and find me,' it seemed to say, 'you'll never know unless you come and find me.' There was a blue spotlight on me and I was all spangly and sparkly – I could feel that I looked magical, and then the box closed, and when it opened I was gone.

"Moe was very sweet; he used to keep champagne in the fridge at Mrs Whitby's and we'd have it with our fish and chips. Sometimes there were fireworks high in the sky over the sea, going up with a great whoosh and exploding into showers of stars and turning the clouds all kinds of colours as if there really might be a heaven up there. Moe wanted there to be magic, he wanted a moment to last indefinitely but moments don't do that. He loved fooling the punters with his illusions while I stood around and looked pretty but seaside hotels are dreary places and after a while I won't be young and pretty any more and then what? Do your parents love each other?"

"Of course they do."

"Do they look after each other in sickness and in health and do they look after you and keep things going and pay the bills and call the plumber and everything like that?"

"Yes." I was thinking of Mum playing 'Claire de Lune' and trying to get it right and I was thinking of Dad in the little would worrying about her.

"Life is something you can drown in if you're not a strong swimmer," said Zelda. "I'm not and I need someone who is, someone who can save me when I'm going down for the third time. Moe wasn't that man, neither was the one before him. Maybe twenty years from now I'll be sorry but I don't think so."

"I think maybe Moe Nagic was the one who needed a strong swimmer to save him," I said.

Zelda put her hand over my mouth. "Don't say any more. I've got to go now, Charles is waiting for me down by the road but I don't know how to get back there."

"I'll show you." She was so beautiful, so delicate – the sort of woman you'd want to take care of and protect from all harm. I took her hand again and we went through the trees and down the hill to the brudge and that bit of road off to the side that I'd never noticed. There was Charles with his Jaguar with its top down. We nodded to each other from a distance but Zelda didn't introduce us.

"Goodbye, Nick," she said, and kissed me on the mouth. Her lips were rose-petal soft – I can still feel that kiss and I can almost smell her perfume. Then she got into the Jaguar and drove off with Charles and I stood there smelling the exhaust while the car got smaller and smaller in the distance. I said to my mind, I'm not ready for all this grownup stuff.

NEITHER ARE THE GROWNUPS BUT THAT'S LIFE.

What now?

THERE'S STILL THE LITTLE WOULD TO DO.

I started up the hill again, through the misshapen trees and twisty spaces, through the dead leaves and the soggy newspapers and the used condoms, thinking about Zelda Watson. The Zelda I'd seen was from the seventies – she'd be about Mum's age by now. I wondered where she was and what she was doing. I wondered if, in some other picture world somewhere, someone was seeing me as I'd be twenty years from now. Crazy thought. I remembered then that I hadn't asked Zelda why she'd so disliked the watercolour of the old brudge and I wished I had.

When I got to the top of the hill there was Mum in a white dress. She was sitting cross-legged at the base of a tree, leaning her head on her hand and looking thoughtful.

"Mum," I said, "are you all right?"

"I don't know," she said. "Maybe a little less than half

72

right and a little more than half wrong. Little would I have thought that after all these years I'd still be here. You'd expect a woman of any intelligence to have found her way out by now."

"I don't understand, Mum. How could you be stuck in this little would for so many years?"

"That's what I keep asking myself. Nick, if you saw me in the tube or on a bus and I wasn't your mother, would you think, 'I wonder who she is?' or would you maybe not notice me at all?"

"I don't know. I don't always notice people in the tube or on buses."

"Very tactful. Before I met your father I was going with a young man who was a bassoonist with the London Philharmonic. He said I was the most interesting woman he'd ever met. We used to read to each other in bed. We did *A la Recherche du Temps Perdu* in the original French. With champagne and caviare. One Valentine's day he hired a pilot to skywrite ALBERT LOVES VIOLET over Kilburn which was where I lived at the time. Have I told you that I used to be a secondary school teacher?"

"Yes, Mum, you have."

"They called me Miss Stevens and I had all kinds of things in my head that aren't there any more:

> 'On either side the river lie
> Long fields of barley and of rye,
> That clothe the wold and meet the sky;
> And thro' the field the road runs by
>   To many-tower'd Camelot...'

I used to know the whole of *The Lady of Shalott*, would

you believe it? Now more than half of it's gone. I can remember a time when I'd wake up in the morning and I'd think: anything can happen. If I closed my eyes I'd see brilliant colours in the darkness. Where does it go, the magic?"

"Mum, do you want to come with me? I think I can find a way out of the little would."

"No, Nick, you go ahead – this is something I've got to do alone. I'll probably see you later back at the house."

"Mum, I don't understand: one moment you say you've been stuck here for years and the next you say you'll see me back at the house."

"You'll understand when you're older: when you're grown up there's nothing unusual about spending a good bit of your time lost in the wood and the rest of it doing whatever you ordinarily do."

"I've seen Dad here, you know. He was looking for you."

"I know. He'll find me soon enough but for the moment I like being alone. Don't worry about me, I'll be fine. See you (suddenly she wasn't there) later."

I looked down and saw my feet walking uphill again.

NICE WOMAN, YOUR MOTHER, said my mind.

Yes, I said, she is. But you know, I'd just as soon not have my family here in the juzzle world. I almost can't remember any more how this whole thing started but I know I wanted it to be separate from everything else.

YOU'RE ALMOST THIRTEEN, NICK. YOU'RE OLD ENOUGH TO UNDERSTAND WHAT I'M GOING TO TELL YOU.

What?

THERE ARE NO SEPARATE THINGS.

By then the trees were thinning out and I could see

open sky beyond when I reached the top of the hill and started down the other side and out of the little would. As I walked I thought about Mum and the bassoonist and I heard in my head *'Claire de Lune'*, played hesitantly but with a light touch.

6

The Mise

Now the little would was behind me and still there was no sign of Cynthia. I hadn't attempted a thorough sweep search because all the time I'd been in among the trees I'd had the feeling she was somewhere straight ahead, not off to either side. Coming down the hill I found myself on a track that led on to a plain. Is this the Trokeville Way? I wondered. It was getting on for evening and I was hoping for lights in the distance but there were none to be seen.

Ahead of me down on the lower ground I saw some sort of earthworks: three circular grassy ramparts arranged concentrically with ditches between them. The outer circle was about a hundred and fifty metres across. Each of the earthen rings had seven gaps in it so placed that you couldn't go straight to the centre – when you went through the first opening you'd have to turn right or left to find the next. It was so simple that it could hardly be called a maze: a few turns to the right or left would take you to the centre and out the other side. Strange, I thought, as the music of '*Libertango*' started playing itself in my head – I've seen this place before. The look of the mise reminded me of a long-ago family outing in Dorset when we visited Maiden Castle and saw great earthen ramparts and ditches at the entrance, possibly put there to baffle invaders. Dad had said they made him think of female genitalia, Mum said he had just one thing on his mind, and I asked who the Genitalia were; I thought they might be an Iron Age tribe.

As I got closer I saw that the space between the ramparts were V-shaped in section, and from the bottom of each V to the top of its rampart must have been about thirty feet, so that climbing to the top of the first one wouldn't give a complete view of what was beyond it.

By the time I reached the base of the first rampart the last of the twilight was gone and in the darkness the mise seemed to be brooding over its secrets, seemed not to want intruders. From the little would on the hill behind me came the calling of the owls again. It seemed a very long time since I'd first heard those owls on the old brudge and I was feeling very tired.

ME TOO, said my mind.

What?

TIRED, VERY TIRED.

We've got to find Cynthia. Either she's in the mise or somewhere beyond it.

I DON'T KNOW HOW MUCH LONGER I CAN HOLD THIS TOGETHER.

But you told me just a little while ago you were stuck in this mode!

FOR AS LONG AS I CAN HOLD IT TOGETHER BUT I'M VERY, VERY TIRED.

The dark ramparts before me seemed to waver. Silent, in wild surmise, I saw for a moment the heave and swell of the blue Pacific. Almost I could smell the sea. You can't let go now, I said to my mind.

No answer.

How can the earth be so much like the sea. Does it mean something?

Again no answer, only the heave and swell of the ground under my feet. Now I could see the moon through a parting in the clouds – a full moon, like a woman in a white nightdress. I climbed to the top of the first rampart and made a complete circuit of it. The ditch was clearly visible in the moonlight but I couldn't see anyone. "Cynthia!" I called. "Are you in there?"

No answer. I sat there on the ancient grass at the top of the rampart that was still warm from the heat of the day and I smelled the earth and now that I'd spoken her name in this place everything was different. I closed my eyes and it seemed that the moonlight was in my head and in the moonlight I saw Cynthia's face, her great luminous eyes full of a mystery that I'd never understand. And even then, as young as I was, I knew that it wasn't meant to be understood – all I could do was offer myself to it. The ancient earthen circles of the mise now seemed inseparable from that mystery and her presence was all around me, rising with the evening mist.

The moon was fading, the earth and the sea. "No!" I shouted, because I knew then that this place and this time would never happen again, knew that if I lost the mise it was lost for ever. I came down the inside of the first rampart into the ditch. I seemed to feel centuries pressing on me, my ears began to hum, and the moonlight filled up with darkness. "Only three!" I said to the darkness, "Only three circles!" I was so afraid that my mind might let go of everything. But even as I said that I knew there would be many, many circles in this mise: the three ramparts I had first seen had only been an illusion to lure me into this darkness. I tried to sense Cynthia's physical presence again but it was gone and all I could feel was that I had to go through the mise to find her.

It was hard to keep from panicking because now I sensed that each moment might be the last of the juzzle world, it wouldn't ever be there again however many times I spun the gyroscope – I cursed Moe Nagic for not telling me that. Maybe he hadn't known; maybe he'd never got this far into the juzzle world.

I made a complete circuit of each ditch, going always to the left. When I reached the first gap I saw that the next ditch was about half a metre lower than the ground I stood on. I jumped down into it, took off my pyjama top, laid it in the gap to mark my place, and ran all the way around the ditch. When I reached the pyjama top again I picked it up, went to the first gap in the next rampart, jumped down to the next level, turned left, and repeated the process. Strange, I thought, I've seen this place before. Or maybe it's the only place there is but it doesn't always look the same.

On the next level I was about halfway around when I almost ran into someone who was sitting on the ground with his back against the rampart. "Always in a hurry, Hartley," he said in a mournful voice. It was Mr Vickers, our History teacher. I haven't mentioned him before this because there was never any need to.

"Mr Vickers," I said, as we rose and fell in the dark-

ness below the moonlight, sometimes fading and sometimes not. "Sir," I said, "what are you mising here?
Doing, rather."

"What am I doing here? I should have thought you
might have surmised that I am talking to you. Stand still
and stop fidgeting."

"Look, Sir," I said, "I'm awfully sorry but I really
haven't the time to talk to you now."

"What's this, role reversal? I'm the one who hasn't the
time to talk to you but I'm taking the time and you'll
jolly well do the listening."

"Sir."

"How many years did Charles I rule without a par-
liament?"

"Eleven, Sir."

"Eleven years, and in your essay of last October on
the events leading up to the Great Rebellion you gave
those eleven years one line. You wrote: 'In the eleven
years that Charles ruled without parliaments things
went from bad to worse.' Nothing at all about ship-
money, nothing at all about a great many things." Mr
Vickers was a miserable-looking man with a face like a
bloodhound and he seemed to be enjoying his misery
as he continued his sermon. "An intensely interesting
period in our history failed to stir you to more than
fifteen words. Was this a failure of intelligence, of under-
standing? I think not. Was it simple laziness? Laziness
is never simple. What we have to deal with here is
nothing less than a failure of the will, a disinclination to
press home the argument. What we have here may well
be a slackness of character. Pay attention, Hartley: do

better." He shook a finger at me and slid into the shadows.

Did you have to do that? I said to my mind. While I was being lectured by Vickers Cynthia could have gone past me and I wouldn't have known. And Buncher's probably back from hospital and following her by now.

I'VE TOLD YOU – I'M NOT SURE HOW MUCH LONGER I CAN HOLD THIS TOGETHER, AND I'M TOO TIRED TO SHUT OUT EVERYTHING ELSE.

As I circled and circled, always going deeper, I kept looking up, hoping for a glimmer of the moon trailing her white nightdress through the clouds but there was only darkness. I felt the cold fear rising in my stomach like the chill that comes up from the sea when you swim out into deep water, and now the fear was not only that my mind would let go of the juzzle world but that it would let go of me as well.

I stopped counting the ramparts and ditches and just hurried on, desperate to find Cynthia. The narrowing circles of the mise gave it a shape like a downward-pointing woman's breast. The darkness had a femaleness about it so that even though I was afraid of the mise I was enticed by the smell of the earth and its warm breath on me. I gave myself to the mystery of it, let myself be easy with it until the deep sea-chill faded and the fear was gone but I was so worn out that I had to stop running. The mise must have been at least three times as deep as Nelson's column is tall and the circles didn't seem to be getting much smaller.

I leant my back against a rampart and let myself slide down until I was sitting on the ground with my legs drawn up, my arms resting on my knees and my head resting on my arms. I think I might have given up right there if I hadn't been so afraid that my mind might let go of me. I could see the headline: MIND LOSES BOY, and I began to laugh; maybe I was hysterical by then. Someone was weeping nearby. Cynthia? It didn't sound like a girl. Buncher? I got up and followed the sound to the left around the curve of the ditch. There was a man sitting in the same position I'd been in a few moments ago. White hat, white T-shirt, jeans, tennis shoes – I recognised him as the painter I'd met down by the old brudge. "What are you crying about?" I said.

He looked up with his face that just looked like any-body at all. Or nobody. "It doesn't go away," he said.

"What doesn't go away?"

"The pain."

"What pain?"

"The pain of life."

"Life in general or a particular part of it?"

"That bridge back there in the foreground of this pic-ture, that's where we used to meet."

"Who?"

"Her name was Zelda."

"Zelda Watson?"

"Yes. You know her then?"

"I met her back in the little would."

"I wanted to marry her but one evening on that bridge she told me she was leaving me for someone else. The next day I went back there and put an end to myself."

"How did you do it?" I'm always interest in the practi-cal details of life and death.

"Twelve-bore shotgun. Now I'm gone but the pain

isn't. I was nobody then and I'm even more nobody now but the pain and my failure are still here."

"What was your failure?"

"I never found out who I was."

"Could you explain that, please?"

"My parents wanted me to be . . ." he paused.

"What? What did they want you to be?"

"Something else . . . a barrister. Yes, a barrister."

"And?"

"In the second or third year of my course I saw that I was never going to be any good at Law: I was more interested in things that had no precedents, I wanted my life to be full of the unpredictable. I'd always painted a bit and I thought I might do something in that line so I dropped Law and took up Art. I did better with that; I got my degree, found a teaching post somewhere in the provinces, got a few commissions, was rejected two or three times by the Royal Academy, and found that I'd gone as far as I could. I was reasonably competent and every now and then I sold a picture but I knew I was never going to be as good as I wanted to be."

"Then you *did* find out who you were: you were a not-good-enough-painter."

"That's one way of looking at it, I suppose. I had the teaching post and enough to live on and I settled into a life of disappointment. Then I met a Zelda and fell in love with her. She was so beautiful! She was like a diamond with glinting coloured lights, she was magical. When I was with her I felt as if I was going to find the real me and everything would be better."

"Was it?"

"It was for a while, then she said there was no magic

83

in our life together and she left me for a man who did tricks on the stage."

"Moe Nagic?"

"Yes. Is she still with him?"

"No."

"Good. I found out where they'd be staying in Brighton and I paid the landlady to hang *The Old Brudge* in their room, for Zelda to remember me by. Then I went back to the old brudge and shot myself."

"But the pain still hasn't gone away!"

"No, it hasn't. I was a fool to think it would. Pain is something that's always there, like gravity. She was like a diamond glinting in the dark and always just out of reach, even when I was holding her. Why are you here?"

"I'm looking for a girl who came this way, I think."

"Is she like a diamond?"

"She's like the girl in the Burne-Jones painting, *King Cophetua and the Beggar Maid*."

"As beautiful as that!"

"Yes."

"As dark and strange and mysterious and magical as that?"

"Yes."

"And you love her?"

"Yes."

"In the Tennyson poem that inspired Burne-Jones, King Cophetua made the beggar maid his queen."

"I know:

As shines the moon in clouded skies,
    She in her poor attire was seen:
One praised her ancles, one her eyes,

84

One her dark hair and lovesome mien.
So sweet her face, such angel grace,
  In all that land had never been:
Cophetua sware a royal oath:
  'This beggar maid shall be my queen!' "

"Do you think they were happy together?" said the painter.

"I don't know. I don't think he was her equal."

"In what way?"

"She was something beyond him – you can see it in her eyes."

"Something ungraspable, like a diamond in the dark, full of brilliant light but you reach for it and it isn't there?"

"Maybe."

"This girl you love, what's her name?"

"Cynthia."

"Are you her equal? Are you dark and strange and mysterious and magical?"

"I'm strange."

"Is she something beyond you?"

"Maybe."

"Have you ever kissed her?"

"No."

"Touched her, held her hand?"

"No. I was in a dream she had."

"What did you do in the dream?"

"I was on the brudge that's in your watercolour and I saw her in the little would."

"And that's why you came into this picture? You

couldn't approach her in ordinary reality so you thought you could do it here?"

"Well, actually there were other reasons."

"What reasons?"

"I'd lost another fight with Harry Buncher and I wanted to do better."

"Buncher was the boy with the bloody head, the one you put in my car?"

"Yes."

"Looked as if you won that fight."

"With a shovel, here in the little would. I think I still have to do better back in the regular world."

"Think you'll get out of here?"

"I hope so."

"*I* never did."

"Maybe you didn't want to badly enough."

"But you do, eh?"

"Yes."

"Was that you I heard laughing a while ago?"

"Probably."

"Sounded a little crazy."

"I am a little crazy, I think."

"Maybe that's what it takes to get out of here. Good luck."

"Thanks. I forgot to ask you: why did you call it a *brudge* instead of a bridge?"

"Because that was where my happiness was begrudged me."

"Wait, before you disappear – you've never told me your name."

"I'm nobody, really," and he wasn't there any more.

I carried on and the darkness deepened. I sensed that

I was getting close to the centre of the mise and I could feel a tension in the air, as if something was about to happen. I could well understand how difficult it must be for my mind to hold all this together because by now I scarcely knew which way was up. My head was full of confused images and words and my senses were here and elsewhere – I saw the wild surmise of the blue Pacific so wide and far and deep from my peak below the full moon in her white nightdress; I saw the distant glimmer of Zelda, no, of Cynthia, smelled the scent of her hair, heard her voice but couldn't make out what she was saying, and all the while there was a desperate hurrying in me to find her before the mise vanished and took me with it.

Then I heard crying again. "O God," I said. "Please give me a break and don't make me stop to talk to anybody else now!" I knew of course that my mind could no longer keep out whatever wanted to come in so all I could do was hope that this next encounter would be brief. Until now it had still been possible to see the ditches and ramparts and my pyjama-top marker. Now, however, the darkness was complete: I couldn't see anything at all. With my hands outstretched to feel my way around the rampart I moved carefully forward. "Who's there?" I said.

"It's me – Richie. I'm lost in the dark and I'm scared."

Richie Patel! He'd arrived at Castleford Court two years ago; his father was in the diplomatic service and they'd moved about a lot. Richie was in my year and he had a hard time of it. He was small and timid, an outsider always hoping to be accepted by the insiders – what you might call a classic victim type. He was no good at sports, afraid of water, afraid of heights – he was a little bundle of anxiety. Being something of an outsider myself I befriended Richie. He looked on me as his advisor and protector and I have to admit that that made me feel big.

One weekend Bill Wiggins invited Tom Jeffreys and Oliver Broughton and me to sleep over at his place on Friday night. Then, surprisingly, because he hadn't been at all friendly to him before that, he invited Richie as well. Richie's face lit up – he finally felt that he belonged. That Friday it was pouring with rain, which made the indoors that much more cosy; Bill's parents and his older sister Agnes were out for the evening so we had the house to ourselves.

Bill had money for pizza and Agnes had very kindly got *A Nightmare on Elm Street* (18) out of the video shop for us so the evening looked like being a satisfactory one. We ordered three X-large pizzas with pepperoni, anchovies, and black olives, garlic bread, and three 1.5 litre bottles of Coke and when they arrived we settled down to serious enjoyment of the video. I myself have never found a scary film that scared me and Bill and Tom and Oliver were pretty much the same but Richie had to cover his eyes when things got too bloody, and he said, "Oh, no!" when Freddie Kreuger's blade-fingered hand came up out of the water between the legs of the girl in the bath.

When we finished the film Bill said he had a great idea for rounding off the evening. He winked at the rest of us and said to Richie, "Tom and Nick and Oliver and I have a little club. Would you like to be a member?"

"Yes," said Richie, "I would."

"There's a thing you have to do for initiation."

"What's that?"

"You have to spend an hour alone in the murder room."

"Where's the murder room?" said Richie, and there was a little quaver in his voice.

"It's an empty house just down the road, by the river. Some people say the place is haunted but it's just an empty house that two people got killed in. A woman and her lover were found in bed by her husband and he stabbed them both to death. There was blood all over and on wet nights you can still smell it. If you want to be in our club you have to stay in there for an hour by yourself."

"Just one hour and then you'll come and get me?"

"Promise."

"And the house isn't really haunted, is it?"

"I don't think so," said Bill. "You know how people make up stories about places where there's been a murder."

"OK," said Richie. "Just one hour."

So we all went out into the rainy night and took Richie down the road to the empty house. It was a tall narrow house with a tower at one end and it stood alone by the river with three estate agents' signs making it look as if nobody wanted to buy it. Off to the right was the Putney Bridge with its lamps and the lights of cars crossing it. The rain and the sound of the cars in the distance made the place seem even more isolated and all the black windows looked as if they were taking notice of us. There was a hedge all round and an iron gate which clanged shut behind us. "This place *looks* haunted," said Richie.

"Sometimes you hear things," said Bill, "but we've never seen anything, have we?"

"One time I thought I saw something out of the corner of my eye," said Oliver, "but I wasn't sure."

"What did it look like?" said Richie.

"I couldn't see its face," said Oliver. "It was crawling on its hands and knees. Maybe it was a cat."

We got in round the back through a window with a broken lock. Bill had a torch and he moved the circle of light over the bare floors and empty walls. The house had a musty smell. "The murder room's on the top floor," he said, and we followed him up the stairs with Richie holding on to my jacket.

When we got to the top floor Bill led us to a closed door. When we opened it we saw again the lights of Putney Bridge through the two windows. The light from the torch made the darkness in the room seem darker. Richie tried the wall switch but the electricity had been turned off. "Is this the room?" he said.

"Yes," said Bill.

"I can smell the blood," said Richie.

"We'll be back for you in an hour," said Bill.

"Stay in this room, Richie," I said. "Don't go rushing about."

"Can I have the torch, please?" said Richie.

"Sorry," said Bill, "the rules are that you have to be alone without a light. Good luck. See you in an hour."

"Don't be late," said Richie.

The rest of us went back to Bill's house and sat down to watch *A Nightmare on Elm Street* again. I said to Bill,

"Why did you invite Richie and then make up all that crap about an initiation and a haunted house? Nobody ever got murdered in that place."

"I don't know – he's such a little creep that it just came into my head to do it. Probably do him good, really, make him pull himself together, not be such a baby."

I couldn't help worrying about Richie, however, and I convinced Bill that we ought to go back for him after fifteen minutes. When the two of us got to the house Bill said, "We don't want to startle him with any sudden noise," so we crept up the stairs as silently as possible and Bill went to the room next to the one Richie was in. I tried to pull him away to steer him to the right door but he shook his head and whispered to me to be quiet. Then he put his face next to the wall and began to make sounds like a woman having sex, sighing and groaning as if a tremendous orgasm was about to happen. I punched him but he clapped a hand over my mouth and kept on with his sound effects.

It couldn't have been more than half a second till I flung his hand away but by then we heard Richie in the next room, say, "Oh, my God! The dead ones are back!" and he rushed out of there and fell down the stairs. When we got to him he was unconscious.

Bill left me the torch and ran back to his house to phone for an ambulance while I stayed with Richie, patting his face and hoping to bring him around. After a while he opened his eyes and said, "Dead people making love."

"No," I said, "that was Bill's idea of a joke."

"Bloody little wog," said Richie.

"Who?"

"Back where came from. Go. Smell blood."

"There wasn't any blood, no one got murdered there – Bill made it all up."

"Leg." His left leg was twisted under him and I thought it was probably broken. I was afraid of doing more damage but I tried to hold it together where the break seemed to be and very gently moved it to a more comfortable position.

"Such good," said Richie, "friend."

By then Bill was back to tell us that he'd be waiting for the ambulance down on the road. "If they ask how it happened let's just say we were exploring the house and he fell down the stairs," he said to me.

"Such good," said Richie.

This being Friday night there was a long wait for the ambulance but eventually two paramedics named Brenda and Jack arrived, put a splint on Richie's leg, and off we went to Queen Mary's A & E with siren and flashers going while Bill stayed behind to phone Richie's parents.

At Queen Mary's I waited in the reception area while they took Richie inside. On my left was a tall woman of eighty or so with a fringe and a ponytail, sweatshirt, jeans, and trainers, who looked as if she'd been in a fight. She said she'd been watching *The Vanishing* for the third time. "I started upstairs still thinking about it," she said, "trod on the cat, leapt back, lost my footing, crashed into the newel post, and seem to have broken my nose. Horrific film! Imagine – you open your eyes and you're looking up at the lid of your coffin! Buried alive!"

On my right was a man with blood all down one side of his face who wanted a light and got impatient with me when I said we were in a no-smoking area. He breathed the fumes of whatever he'd been drinking on me and reprimanded me for being a smartarse kid. "When I was a kid..." he said, and seemed to forget what he was going to say. "When I was a kid," he said finally, "I had the whole world in front of me. What d'you think of that, hey?"

I had no comeback whatever and he wobbled away to the other side of the reception area where he eventually got a light and sat down and muttered to himself. The fluorescent units in the ceiling gave the place a kind of bright dullness and one of them kept flickering and buzzing. That and the sound of the drunk's voice have stayed in my mind ever since as belonging to a place that's always waiting on the other side of the everyday allrightness which is as thin as tissue paper and very easy to fall through if you're not careful.

After Richie's mum and dad arrived and had seen Richie they told me he'd have to stay overnight for observation but the doctor had said he'd be all right. Mrs Patel was very pleased that Richie had made new friends but hoped we'd be more careful in future. Mr Patel said that boys were adventurous and we could be thankful that it was nothing worse than a broken leg and a concussion. I went in and said goodbye to Richie and then the Patels drove me back to Bill's house.

When I got home the next afternoon Mum and Dad had already heard the Bill version from Mr and Mrs Wiggins and they tried to get more information out of me but I stuck to our story and was let off with nothing worse than a short lecture on responsibility.

I was less friendly with Bill and Oliver after that, and when Richie came back to school I found that I'd rather lost interest in him. He was over to play chess a couple of times and once I was invited to lunch at his place and we went to the pictures but that was about it. He was only at Castleford Court for a year, then the family moved and we said we'd write but I wasn't very good about answering his letters and that fizzled out. And this was the Richie Patel who'd turned up in the mise now, sitting in the dark and crying.

"Richie," I said. "What brings you here?"

"I don't know. I got lost in the dark and here I am."

"I know the feeling. Listen, Richie, this isn't really happening and you're not really here: it's a mind trip and people keep turning up and disappearing, which is what you'll do in a moment. I've got to be moving along now. See you."

"I don't know how to disappear," said Richie.

"Everybody else did."

"How did they do it?"

"I don't know. One moment they're here and the next they're not. Try."

"I'm trying but nothing happens. Can't I come with you?"

I didn't want to be lumbered with him but I couldn't very well leave him there. "All right," I said, "let's go then."

"Aren't you scared?"

"I was scared a while back but I'm not now."

"How do you not be scared?"

I remembered when I'd stopped being scared. It hadn't been that long ago actually. "If you can tune into the darkness," I said, "if you can stop being separate from it the fear goes away." I explained my pyjama-top system to Richie and started off round the ditch with him holding on to my hand.

When we came back to the pyjama top we went through the gap and jumped down to the next level. In the air on my face I could feel that the space we were in was more open than before. I felt around for the next rampart and it wasn't there. I put my pyjama top back on and we walked out towards the far side of the circular space that was the bottom of the mise. I paced off about fifty metres from one side to the other. "Anybody here besides Richie and me?" I said.

No answer. I looked up and far, far away I saw the moon in the great dark circle of the mise. It was light enough for Richie and me to see each other. He was wearing school uniform. "How come you're not dressed," he said.

"That's a long story, Richie. We can talk about it later. Now all we have to do is go up and out."

"It's so dark here."

"No, it isn't – look at the moon shining down on us."

"It's still dark in here. I hate stumbling around in the dark, I keep remembering how I fell down the stairs in the haunted house."

"Well, you can't fall down more than one step here, so let's just push on." As we climbed I didn't bother with another circuit of each level – I knew that Cynthia had either cruised straight through the mise without the time-consuming encounters I'd had and was far ahead of me or she'd simply bypassed it and gone home by now. My blue Pacific! I said to my mind; my wild surmise – where is it? The moon is so far away!

WHAT ARE YOU TALKING ABOUT?

I'm not sure. I came into the mise for Cynthia Jeffreys and I found my History teacher, then the painter who did this picture I'm in, then Richie Patel. The others disappeared after I talked to them but Richie's still with me. This mise thing, what's it all about – can you tell me?

YOU KEEP NAGGING ME FOR ANSWERS. DO YOU REALISE THE KIND OF EFFORT IT TAKES TO KEEP THIS WHOLE THING TOGETHER WHILE YOU BUMBLE AROUND IN IT? ANSWERS ARE NOT MY BUSINESS. I'VE GOT THE WHOLE WORLD IN ME BUT I DON'T KNOW WHAT ANY OF IT MEANS, ALL RIGHT?

You *what*?

WHAT?

You've got the whole world in you and you don't know what any of it means?

THAT'S WHAT I SAID.

Now you tell me!

So?

So how can you not know what it means? You're my mind, for God's sake!

WHAT, YOU WANT EVERYTHING TO BE HANDED TO YOU ON A PLATE? I'M GIVING YOU THE WORLD. WHAT IT MEANS IS YOUR PROBLEM AND HOW YOU DEAL WITH IT IS YOUR PROBLEM, OK?

Jesus! My parents are lost in the would and my mind doesn't know what anything means. How am I supposed to get from here to the rest of my life?

HOWEVER YOU CAN.

7

What About The Troke?

"OK," I said to Richie. "Let's go." Through the gap that was in front of us I saw open space. As we scrambled up to ground level Richie slipped and fell. "Are you all right?" I said as I helped him up.

"Shit!" he said. "I've twisted my ankle. It's the same leg I broke when I fell down the stairs in the haunted house."

"Can you stand on it?"

"Not really."

I helped him up through the gap and we were out in the open. In the distance ahead I saw the lights of a town. They didn't look any more than a couple of miles away.

"What place is that?" said Richie.

"Trokeville, I think." I felt a surge of annoyance sweep over me because I was looking at it with Richie when I wanted to be alone.

SOME OF THEM WILL BE WITH YOU ALL OF THE TIME AND ALL OF THEM WILL BE WITH YOU SOME OF THE TIME, said my mind.

What? I said. Are you giving me answers now?

JUST TELLING YOU HOW IT IS.

Richie's arm was around my shoulders so he could use me as a crutch and his weight was dragging me down and pressing my bare feet on to every pebble and sharp thing on the ground. I couldn't help thinking that he was enjoying being a burden to me. "Are we going to Trokeville?" he said.

"We're going to whatever comes next, Richie. Around here you never know."

"Nick?"

"What?"

"Why didn't you answer my last two letters?"

"I'm not much of a letter writer, Richie."

"I thought you were my friend."

I made some kind of a sound that could have been whatever he wanted it to be.

"How come you're walking around in your pyjamas?" he said. "You were going to tell me about that."

"Right now I don't think I've got the strength for it. Let's just save our breath and try to keep moving." By now the track had become a metalled road with a white line down the centre of it and Harry Buncher standing by the side of it.

"Oh, for Christ's sake, you again," he said.

"Did you go through the mise?" I said.

"What's the mise?"

"That thing with the circular ramparts and ditches."

"Why would I go through that? I went around it."

"Hi, Harry," said Richie.

"Where'd you find *him*?" said Harry to me.

"Doesn't matter. Where's Cynthia?"

"That's what I'd like to know – I was hoping for a bit

of that but this whole thing has been a big waste of time as far as I'm concerned."

"My heart bleeds for you. Help me with Richie."

"What if I say no?"

"Listen, Buncher, if you want to get out of here you're jolly well going to have to do your part like the rest of us."

"Says who?"

"I think that's just how it is. If you want to take your chance alone, go ahead."

Buncher took Richie's other arm over his shoulder. "You're a real pain in the arse, do you know that?" he said.

"You're not much of a fun guy either, Harry." Then we both kept quiet and concentrated on hauling Richie along. It wasn't night any more but a grey dawn with mist rising from the fields on either side. I hadn't noticed fields before. There was no town visible where last night's lights had been. No road signs either. No birds to be seen or heard, only silence and greyness. After a while I stopped looking ahead and walked with my head down, watching my sore and bleeding feet moving forward and back.

"Aha!" said Harry. I looked up and there was Cynthia standing by the road in a white nightdress. Harry flung off Richie's arm and I thought he was going to make a rush at Cynthia but all he did was try to brush off some of the black muck that had dried on his pyjamas. His face was very red.

"Hi," said Cynthia.

"Hi," said the three of us.

"I'd like to talk to Nick alone for a moment, please," said Cynthia.

"Of course," said Richie. Harry nodded and he and Richie sat down by the side of the road while Cynthia and I walked on a little way. There was a breeze that pressed her thin nightdress against her body. I told myself to look away but I couldn't. "Did you go through the mise?" I said. "You know, the round thing with the ramparts and ditches?"

"That place looked very scary to me so I just walked around it. Did you go into it?"

"Yes, I did, and it took me a long time to get out of it."

"Poor Nick! You do everything the hard way, don't you?"

"I guess so. What about Buncher? Did you run into him at all?"

"Very strange, that boy – he was following me at a distance for a long time, then I stopped and asked him what he wanted and he turned and walked away. I think he must be very bashful with girls. Is he?"

"I wouldn't know, really. You wanted to talk to me?"

"Yes." She hesitated. "This is embarrassing." She put her hand on my arm and her hair swung against my face.

"What is?" The sun was high now and there was a flat glare on everything. No cars and no dogs but I seemed to smell exhaust fumes and dogshit baking in the sun.

"I don't know how to begin." She looked at me with those wonderful grey luminous eyes so full of mystery and I went weak in the knees. As always her eyes reminded me of the beggar maid in the Burne-Jones painting but there was something else at the back of my mind, something I was trying to remember and couldn't. "I know this is some special kind of reality," she said, "and I think I'm here because you like me. Am I right?"

I nodded; I was too choked up to speak. She took my hand and the thrill of it went all through me.

"How can I say this in the least hurtful way?" she said.

"Just say it, Cynthia."

"Girls mature faster than boys – probably you know that, yes?"

"Yes."

"I'm more than a year older than you, Nick, and I've got a boyfriend."

"How old is he?"

"Fifteen."

"Oh." I let my hand slide away from hers.

"You're very sweet, Nick, and I really like you but that's how it is." She kissed me on the mouth, rose-petal lips like Zelda's, and she was gone.

Did you hear that? I said to my mind.

WHAT CAN I TELL YOU? THIS IS REALITY?

On that road where there hadn't been any cars I heard one pulling away and saw a big Mercedes growing small in the distance. No sign of Buncher and Richie so it must have been Richie's dad picking them up and leaving me behind. "Hang on!" I shouted to the silence. "What about the troke?" I said. "What about Trokeville?"

"Trokeville? Is that where you've been?" said the nurse who was bending over me. Lavinia Metcalfe, S.R.N., said her name badge. She looked at her watch

101

and wrote something on a chart. "What sort of a trip have you been on?"

"A long one, it feels likes." I noticed a drip feeding into my left arm. "When did I arrive here?"

"Three days ago."

"Somebody brought me in?"

"Your parents."

"Was I hurt or what?"

"You were in some kind of a trance state, on your hands and knees looking at a jigsaw puzzle, they said. Must have been a fascinating puzzle."

"It was."

At that moment the curtains between me and the bed to my left were slid back and I found myself looking at Harry Buncher with his head all bandaged up. He was doing his absolutely evillest face. "You did this," he said, pointing to his head. "You and your bloody mind tricks."

"How's that?" I said.

"Don't come the innocent with me – you've been sending me dreams. We were fighting in one of them and I knocked a bookshelf off the wall on to my head."

"Must've been some really heavy reading on that shelf, Harry."

"Laugh, you bastard. Wait till we're both out of here and you won't be laughing any more, Nicky boy."

"We'll see who does the laughing, Harry boy," I said as he closed the curtains again. I'm not going to look back over these pages to see if I ever actually said that I was afraid of Buncher but now I'm going to admit that in every one of the three fights we'd had at Castleford Court I *was* afraid. Harry Buncher had definitely had me psyched out. We'd be getting back to our unfinished business before too long and I hoped I could back up my mouth action with my fists.

That afternoon the first visitor to our ward was a very pretty red-haired girl with freckles. The afternoon sunlight through the blinds gave her a golden look. There were four other boys in the ward and three of them sat up and took notice. The fourth had his leg in a cast suspended by pulleys so he took notice lying down. She was carrying a sports bag and wearing a St Ursula's blazer – St Ursula's was Cynthia's school. She looked about two years younger than Cynthia so I guessed she was in the year below me. She smiled at me and said, "Hi," as she passed my bed and went to Buncher's.

The curtains were still closed but I heard her say, "Hi, Harry. I've brought your clothes." He must have told her to keep her voice down then because after that I could only hear murmurs. Then she came out, smiled at me again, and left. In a few minutes the curtains slid back and there was Buncher fully dressed and carrying the sports bag. He gave me a menacing look, said, "This isn't over yet," and sloped off.

The girl, I assumed, was his sister. Amazing, that a boy like him should have a sister like her. I replayed her voice in my head and I liked the sound of it. I wondered what her name was, and while I was doing that Cynthia Jeffreys came into the ward and the other four boys took notice again. Even in that sunlight she had a moonlit look.

"Hi," she said. "Are you OK?"

"Hi, Cynthia. I'm fine. I think they'll send me home as soon as the consultant's had a look at me."

"Tom said you liked ghost stories," she said, and gave me a paperback, *Kwaidan*, by Lafcadio Hearn.

"Thanks, I do." I looked at the flyleaf but it was blank. "Would you write something in it for me?" I said.

She blushed and took out a pen and chewed the end of it for a moment, then she wrote something quickly, closed the book, and gave it back to me. "You ..." she said, looking at me, then she paused, looked away and started again. "I had another dream with you in it. We were talking and I don't remember what I said but you were sad. It wasn't like an ordinary dream. You can do things with your mind, can't you?"

"I don't know. What have I done?"

"Well, this dream – I had the feeling that either you'd come into my dream or got me into your dream in some special way. Is that what happened?"

"Strange things have been happening with me, I'm not always sure what's going on."

"Look, Nick ..." Another pause. "This is embarrassing. She leant close to me and put her hand on my arm and her hair swung against my face.

"What is?" I said.

"I don't know how to begin. Those dreams seemed like a special kind of reality and I think I was there because ..." She took a deep breath. "Because you like me. Am I right?"

I nodded. I was too choked up to speak. She took my hand and the thrill of it went all through me.

"How can I say this in the least hurtful way?" she said.

"Just say it, Cynthia."

"Girls mature faster than boys – probably you know that, yes?"

"Yes."

"I'm more than a year older than you, Nick, and I've got a boyfriend. He's fifteen."

I looked down and noticed that she wasn't holding my hand any more. "Cynthia, do you have the feeling that we've had this conversation before?"

"I'm not sure. Something like that, maybe. Anyhow, I'm glad we've had it. See you, Nick." And she was gone. No kiss, only the scent of her lingering on the air.

I opened *Kwaidan* and looked at the inscription:

> *Strange stories for strange Nick,*
> *Best wishes, C.J.*

That was when I first noticed that the heightened vision I'd had ever since Buncher headed me was gone; the colours of things were ordinary again and the details were however they were, nothing more than that.

The consultant came round then, a tall man with white hair and a military moustache who looked as if he might have led the charge of the Light Brigade. He had a nurse and a squad of young doctors following him. "Hello," he said, "I'm Mr Bridge."

"Brudge," I said, not meaning to – it just slipped out.

"Grudge? No, I haven't got a grudge. Have you?"

"Sorry, I'm a little confused."

"As well you might be." He turned to his following. "This young man was brought in three days ago in a trance state. Stiff as a board – you could have used him as a coffee table. No evidence of drugs." He turned back to me. "How'd you get that lump on your head?"

"I banged into a wall the other day. Could that have done it?"

"Send him down for a scan," he said to one of the doctors. Then he said to me, "You haven't been messing about with self-hypnosis, have you?"

"I wouldn't know how."

"Good. We'll run a few tests and send you home in a day or two." He swept off with his squad and I didn't see him again.

Mum and Dad turned up later with grapes and biscuits and Tennyson's poems. They both looked different – smaller, maybe, and they seemed to be looking at me not in their usual way. "What is it?" I said.

"What?" said Dad.

"You look strange."

"We feel a little strange too," said Mum. "We were worried about you and we've been thinking about you. Are you all right?"

"I'm fine."

"I wanted to destroy that puzzle," said Dad, "but Mum wouldn't let me."

"She was right not to. Don't worry, though – I won't be getting into any more trances."

"You know," said Dad. "In a family you see each other every day and everything seems the same until all of a sudden it isn't the same."

"You can say that again."

"I won't though."

"We mustn't tire you," said Mum. They kissed me and were gone. I ate grapes and biscuits, read Lafcadio

Hearn and Tennyson, had an EEG and a CT scan, was discharged, collected by Mum and Dad, and found myself at home again. In my room the juzzle was on the floor looking like nothing special. I put it in its box and closed the lid.

Mum and Dad, not surprisingly, wanted to know where I'd been and what I'd done in my trance and David asked if I'd brought back any holiday snaps. I said it had been like a dream that you mostly forget as soon as you wake up. I told them selected bits and I had one or two questions myself. When I asked Mum about her pre-Dad days it developed that she'd never had a bassoon-playing boyfriend with whom she read Proust and all the rest of it. What *is* this? I said to my mind. Do you just make up whatever suits your purpose?

NODOBY'S PERFECT.

I waited until I found Dad alone, then I asked him, "When you were my age, did you have any career plans?"

"You mean, did I want to be Assistant Manager of the local Britannia Building Society office when I grew up? Tell me, Nick, do I look to you as if that's what I wanted to be?"

"Well, I mean – there's nothing *wrong* with being that. Only . . ."

"Only what?"

"When I saw you on this mind trip, you told me not to let anything stop me from being something but I couldn't hear what that something was."

He put his hand on my shoulder. "Don't let anything stop you from being whatever you have it in you to be, Nick."

"And you said you wanted to be I don't know what, because I didn't hear the rest of it."

"Maybe I never said the rest of it."

"But *was* there something you wanted to be?"

"People who want to be something and have it in them to be it usually make it happen. People who don't have it in them don't make it happen. What I am is what I had it in me to be, OK?" We talked a little more but that was as far as we got with that subject. Maybe some time I'll find out what it was Dad wanted to be but he hasn't told me yet.

A couple of days after things had got back to normal I had a phone call from guess who? Mrs Jeffreys, Cynthia's mother. Very breathy voice, very intimate telephone manner. "Hello, Nick," she said, "this is Zelda Jeffreys." Zelda! I almost fell over. "How are you?" she said. "Back to normal, I hope?"

"Fine, thanks." There came to mind Moe Nagic's eyes, big and grey and luminous, full of mystery and sadness. "Mrs Jeffreys," I said. "Did you used to be Zelda Watson?"

"I guess I still am, really. People don't change that much. Poor Moe! He wasn't what you might call a strong swimmer in the sea of life."

"No, he wasn't." As I said that I was seeing Cynthia's eyes that were like his.

"So when did you meet him, Nick? And how come *The Old Brudge* ended up with you?"

I told her how I'd bought it from Moe Nagic a few days ago and she said, "Poor Moe!" again.

"He seemed sad when I met him," I said. "I think he must have been sad from the time the two of you broke up. Stop me if I'm getting too personal but did you ever see him again?"

"Funny you should ask that, Nick." With her voice she seemed to be putting her hand on my arm as Cynthia had done. "I did see him by chance years ago and we had lunch for old time's sake."

Almost fifteen years ago, I said to myself but not to her. What a strange thing life is! Moe Nagic did manage one bit of magic in his time after all.

"Actually what I called about, Nick, was *The Old Brudge*. It's funny, when you get older, how you want to revisit certain times in your life, happy ones and sad ones. Could I come and see you and look at the picture?"

"It's a jigsaw puzzle now, remember – it'll probably look strange to you."

"No more than anything else. Can I come over?"

"Certainly."

When she arrived in her Volvo and I saw her get out of the car, still graceful and Zelda-looking (now that I knew her as Moe Nagic's Zelda) and it was me that she came to see, I had the most wonderful feeling of being included in grown-up secrets. She took my hand and it was like being with Zelda in the juzzle world. I took her up to my room and showed her the juzzle – it was looking altogether ordinary and harmless, just a cut-up watercolour – and she shook her head and began to cry. I patted her on the back very tentatively and all of a sudden she was hugging me. "The magic!" she said. "It goes so quickly!" She smelled good and she felt good and her face against mine was rose-petal soft. She was a great hugger and I was enjoying it but I wondered what Mum would have to say if she were to walk in at that moment.

After a while Mrs Jeffreys turned me loose and gave her attention to the juzzle again. "Poor Phillip!" she said.

"Who's Phillip?"

"Phillip Andrews. He's the one who painted that picture. I said goodbye to him on that brudge and he . . ." She began to cry again and reached for my hand.

"Killed himself?"

She nodded.

"With a twelve-bore shotgun?"

She shook her head. "Rope. From a tree near the brudge."

I gave her a tissue and she blew her nose. Two men dead for love of her, I thought. Wow! Cynthia's mother, the Zelda who'd kissed me in the little would! I was having quite a rich fantasy life in those moments and I could feel in my underpants that Mrs Jeffreys had well and truly dragged me across the threshold of puberty. Her brief visit to my room did not, however, end up like those films in which an older woman initiates a boy into the mysteries of sex. Not that I'd have complained if it had done.

Mrs Jeffreys wanted to buy the juzzle but I said no, she must have it as a gift from me and that's why I haven't got it any more. The gyroscope, by the way – when I came home from hospital I'd found it smashed. Maybe I did it myself when I was in that trance, I don't know.

8

Trokeville

A couple of weeks passed and Buncher and I were both about ready to pick up where we'd left off. He was beginning to give me more and more evil looks and I could see that the big event would be coming sooner rather than later. One day in lunch break my mind suddenly spoke up.

YOU KNOW WHAT? it said.

What?

DO IT TO HIM BEFORE HE DOES IT TO YOU.

What do you mean?

TAKE THE INITIATIVE.

What, today? Now?

THERE'S NO TIME LIKE THE PRESENT. DO IT NOW AND GET IT OVER WITH.

"Hey, Buncher!" I heard myself say. He was with his followers and he turned towards me with a look of surprise on his face.

"You want something?" he said.

"That's right. I want you to meet me in Sewell Park after school." My words were echoing in my head and I almost couldn't believe I'd said them. Buncher looked absolutely gobsmacked and it was obvious that he'd expected to be the one to make the challenge in his own good time. His followers seemed impressed and there was a general murmur of excitement in the schoolyard. Tom Jeffreys and Bill Wiggins and Oliver Broughton congratulated me and promised to be there to lend their support.

WELL DONE! said my mind. GOOD LUCK.

Thanks, I said. Is this going to be the troke?

YOU'VE BEEN DOING THE TROKE FOR A WHILE NOW AND YOU JUST HAVE TO KEEP ON DOING IT.

And Trokeville, what about that?

TROKEVILLE IS WHEREVER YOU ARE WHEN YOU DO THE TROKE.

When I heard that I realised that I'd already half-suspected it. I could feel the excitement in my stomach and it was nothing like the fear I used to feel. Just remember, I told myself, you were able to deal with him in the reality of the juzzle world and this time you've already got him worried.

Somehow I got through the afternoon but I was in a private place in my head the whole time, getting ready for the fight. I thought of Dad and wondered again what it was he'd wanted to be. I didn't know whether there'd ever been a Buncher in his life but it came to me that if I didn't finish our unfinished business Buncher would be with me always and I really didn't want that.

The last class was finally over. I nodded to Buncher and we headed for Sewell Park with something like half of our year following us. It was about a half mile down the road, the place we went to for games. Off to one side of the football pitch there was some grass with a shelter and a couple of benches and that's where we did it.

"Well, Nicky boy," said Buncher. "Are you ready for your beating?"

"Action talks, bullshit walks," I said, and I could feel inside me a lovely warm rage humping itself up like a big animal from way, way back and long, long ago. I could feel a silent growl in my throat or maybe I was even doing it out loud, I'm not sure.

School fights usually begin with pushing which leads to grappling and both boys on the ground, each trying for a good enough grip to make the other give up. Buncher was too big and heavy for me to risk wrestling with him – I'd have to keep him off me and do it all with boxing.

I could see that a lot of his confidence was gone – even his smell didn't seem that strong any more and his face was full of doubt. He'd always been easy to hit – I just had to look out for his wild rushes.

"Go on, Nick!" shouted my supporters. "Show him!"

"Here we go, Harry!" yelled the Buncherites. "Here we go, here we go, here we go!"

He came at me with his usual no-style style. I kept him away with my left, then caught him with a good right to the jaw. His head snapped back and I saw fear in his eyes. When he came at me again I bloodied his nose. I knew he'd try to head me then, and when he made his rush I stepped back and brought my fist up into his face before he reached me. When he staggered back I moved in with both hands and before too long he was on the ground. He got up again and I knocked him down again and then he got up on one knee but just stayed there shaking his head.

"Had enough?" I said.

He nodded and a cheer went up for me.

TROKEVILLE, said my mind.

It's a good place to be, I said.

9

Felicity

When I got home after the fight there was the predictable What-happened-to-you? session but nothing could spoil that day for me. That isn't quite the end of my story. The next day after school I was coming down Castleford Road and when I reached Moe Nagic's pitch I stopped and leant against the hoarding hearing 'Libertango' in my head and seeing Zelda all spangled and sparkling under a blue spotlight.

While I was standing there I saw Buncher's sister coming towards me. "Hi," she said.

"Hi," I said.

"I saw you in hospital a couple of weeks ago when I visited Harry. I'm Felicity Buncher."

"I remember you very well."

"You gave my brother a thrashing yesterday."

"I don't know what to say."

"You can say, 'Nice to meet you, Felicity.' "

"Nice to meet you, Felicity. I mean, it really is."

"Nice to meet you too, Nick. Actually Harry seems much nicer today. You play flute, don't you?"

"Yes. Do you play anything?"

"Piano. Maybe we could do the Bach flute and harpsi-chord sonatas some time?"

"I'd like that."

"Shall I come over this Saturday afternoon?"

"Great."

We walked down Castleford Road together until we had to go our separate ways. We started on the flute sonatas that Saturday and the session went very felici-tously. We still play Bach but we've been catching up with the present and lately we've been doing Fauré and Hindemith and transcriptions from Debussy piano works, including 'Claire de Lune' and 'Reverie'.

Those strange mental powers I had when I was involved with the juzzle are long gone but I'm more in touch with that lower level of reality than I used to be. And I'm certainly more aware of the strangeness of everything than I ever was before.

In books and films boys who fight each other often end up friends but that didn't happen with Harry Bun-cher and me. I don't think he ever forgave me for what I did to him in the juzzle world and I never forgave him for how he used to bully me before I learned how to get mad. He went off to boarding school the year after that so he's mostly not around now. I know he doesn't like it that his sister is my girlfriend but he can always look for another reality if he's not happy with this one.

The last time I was at the Jeffreys' house Mr Jeffreys was there. It was the first time I'd seen him since learning that he was the Charles that Zelda went off with when she left Moe Nagic. He has the kind of magic that can pay for a big house in Putney, a BMW and a Volvo and I suppose that's been enough for Zelda all these years.

Except when she needed a long lunch with something else on the menu.

The day that I gave Mrs Jeffreys the juzzle I forgot to ask her where the old brudge was and the name of the river it crossed. I was going to do it the next time I saw her but then I decided not to.